Hotwife of the Month Club: Vol 2

4 First Time Wife Sharing Stories

May Hotwife
June Hotwife
July Hotwife
August Hotwife

Lacey Cross

Twisted Rose
+ PUBLISHING +

Contents

For everyone who lives vicariously through my stories, and to those brave enough to explore their fantasies.

May these pages ignite your imagination and celebrate the beauty of consensual adventure.

May Hotwife

Hotwife of the Month Club 5

Lacey Cross

To those who appreciate the sensual dance between observer and observed, this tantalizing tale is for you.

CHAPTER 1

I take a sip of my chardonnay, savoring the crisp flavor as I relax on the plush sofa in my living room with my four closest friends. Our husbands are downstairs in the gaming room playing their monthly poker game while we enjoy our treasured girls' night upstairs. The conversation flows freely, punctuated by frequent peals of laughter and spicy details about our lives.

June's phone trills loudly and she hushes us with a grin and a wave of her hand. "Hold up, ladies, it's the babysitter."

I look over at my best friend Ana and we both giggle conspiratorially as June shoots us a playful dirty look and gets up from the overstuffed armchair, chatting animatedly with the babysitter. She's saying goodnight to her two young kids. This is also part of our monthly ritual, so I know that next she'll take the phone downstairs so her husband Mark can say goodnight to the little ones as well before rejoining the poker crew.

When June returns a few minutes later with a refilled wine glass, she plops down on the sofa and says in a stage whisper, "I think our husbands are up to something. When I walked into the room, they all completely stopped talking."

Ariel raises one perfectly-shaped eyebrow and leans forward. "Ooh, you think they're hiding some juicy secret from us?"

"Definitely," June confirms with a nod. "They only get super secretive like that when there's some really good gossip they don't want to say in front of us. I wonder what it could be this time…" She takes a long sip of wine, eyes sparkling mischievously over the rim of her glass.

I glance over at Ana, sitting cross-legged on the sofa next to me, and notice her cheeks are pink and she looks distinctly uncomfortable. She's picking nervously at a cocktail napkin and refusing to make eye contact with any of us. Hmm, I wonder what's gotten into her all of a sudden.

"Okay, Ana banana, spill it, girl. What scandalous thing is going on with you?" I coax teasingly, reaching over to poke her leg. "You look guilty as hell right now."

Ana takes a big fortifying gulp of wine, clearly nervous. She hesitates, tucking her hair behind one ear, before blurting out, "Um, well…I gave Max permission to tell the guys what happened on our trip to Cancun last month. I…I slept with someone else. And Max watched me do it."

Holy shit. Shy, sweet Ana is a hotwife now? I'm stunned. Right before her trip, she claimed she could never sleep with any other man besides Max. I feel a surprising twinge of jealousy deep in my gut at her unexpected revelation. So many of our friends are experimenting with the lifestyle these days, and I'm starting to wonder what the hell I'm missing out on.

"Oh my god!" Juliet squeals, bouncing excitedly on the sofa across from us. "What was it like? How did it even happen? I need all the dirty details!"

Ana fidgets with the stem of her wine glass. She has a small secretive smile playing as she remembers. "It was actually Max's idea, if you can believe it. He said he thought it would be really exciting and erotic for both of us. And honestly… it was incredible. A total rush. Scary but thrilling, like riding a roller coaster for the first time."

June scoffs, "Well, I'm guessing you aren't the home-wrecking slut that Debra was claiming when she saw you flirting with that trainer online, huh?"

Debra is the prudish wife in our larger friendship circle and she's been a mega judgmental bitch lately, slut-shaming all our friends who are dipping their toes in the lifestyle. She totally blew up at Ana a few weeks ago on our social media group page after seeing Ana posting some thirsty, flirtatious comments to a handsome male bodybuilder online.

Ana blushes an even deeper shade of pink at the memory, and grins bashfully. "Yeah, about that... Max was actually egging me on to sext with the other guy. He got really turned on watching me do it and telling me what to say."

Well, that's shockingly hot. My body hums in delight as I imagine my sweet, submissive husband Jackson doing the same kinky thing—encouraging me to flirt and sext with a hot, ripped guy online while he watches and gets off on it. There's no fucking way that would ever happen in a million years, but I still get a forbidden little thrill shooting up my spine at the naughty thought.

We all pepper Ana with more questions, fascinated by this peek into her newly adventurous sex life. But soon enough, we hear the men clomping up the basement stairs, the poker game apparently over for the night.

As our friends leave, Jackson stands in the open doorway with his arm wrapped around my waist as we wave goodbye to everyone. He exudes comforting strength, reminding me why he's so perfect for me. He and I have our share of problems and disagreements, just like every other couple, but we've been together since college and it's been a damn good ten years.

As Jackson and I get ready for bed, I can't stop thinking about Ana's confession. I wait until we're under the covers to bring it up.

"So, apparently Ana is now a hotwife," I say cautiously, gauging his reaction.

Jackson grins. "I heard the story. Ana seemed the least likely to go for it of all our friends–well, other than Debra." He snorts. "Can you imagine? Debra would probably complain the entire time and slut-shame herself."

My husband's blunt words send an unexpected yearning straight to my core. But instead of picturing Debra, I vividly imagine that it's me in the scenario—crying out what a dirty cock-hungry slut I am while some gorgeous mystery man with a huge cock rails me... with Jackson watching and stroking himself a few feet away. My entire body flushes with heat and I feel slick wetness between my thighs. Fuck.

I almost laugh out loud at myself and my outrageous fantasy as I pull Jackson closer, encouraging him to lay his head on my breast while I play with his hair. Jackson and I may not have a vanilla relationship behind closed doors, but we've never been open to anything wild outside the bedroom. We initially hooked up in college because I thrilled him by taking the dominant role. He was eager to be my sexy little toy and submit to me. It was never supposed to be a permanent dynamic, but we became addicted to each other and the incredible D/s sex, and well... here we are a decade later, still kinky as ever, and also very much in love.

I'm a switch when it comes to BDSM, and while I adore dominating my sexy submissive husband, over the years I sometimes miss the heady thrill of simply being told to get on my knees and worship a big hard cock—of obeying filthy commands and being used like a willing fucktoy. Occasionally, Jackson takes the dominant role, and I love him for doing it, but it's just not in his nature to do it often, and he doesn't fuck me as hard as I crave. I wouldn't trade my relationship with Jackson for the world, though. He's the peanut butter to my jelly, my perfect match.

We lay in comfortable silence for a few minutes, and all I can think about is the fantasy of Jackson watching another man fuck me hard while I surrender to the erotic bliss of being someone else's fucktoy. Jackson's shirtless, the comforter bunched around his waist, and I enjoy the view of his chest. Jackson could easily overpower me physically if he really wanted to, especially because I'm petite at 5'2" and not exactly Wonder Woman strong. But there's nothing sexier to me than bringing a powerful, masculine man to his knees and knowing that he's choosing to let me control and dominate him. The ultimate act of loving submission.

I'm too turned on to sleep and I boldly slide my hand under his pajama pants, heading straight for his semi-hard cock. He chuckles, his eyes crinkling at the corners, as I grab his hardening member and give it a possessive squeeze.

I caress his length and whisper, "Time to earn the privilege of making me breakfast in the morning, my sexy boy toy."

This is an erotic game we like to play on weekends. He always cooks me a delicious breakfast on Sundays, and I like to make him earn the right first. I lightly run my thumb across the head of his cock, massaging the bead of pre-cum into his shaft as it swells in my hand.

Jackson squirms, his breathing picking up. "What would you like me to do, my gorgeous Mistress?"

I trail my fingertips lower to cup and fondle his balls before running my short fingernails teasingly along the sensitive skin of his inner thighs. "First, my sweet slut is going to get naked and then I'm going to give you something to think about," I promise seductively.

I swear I've never seen him get up and scramble out of his pajama bottoms so quickly before. Someone is very excited to play. I stay in bed and shimmy out of my panties and remove my nightgown. I toss them carelessly to the floor. I'm going for maximum efficiency, and pesky clothing will just get in the way of ravaging my man.

When we're both naked and he's back in bed, I give him my most devilish smile. It's time to test the waters and see what my kinky husband really thinks about so many of our friends trying out the hotwife lifestyle lately.

His breath catches as I wrap my fingers around his shaft and slowly start caressing him. His eyes roll back in bliss and he closes them, surrendering to the pleasure.

"That feels so good," he moans, his voice gravelly from desire. "Don't stop, please."

I still my hand, holding his cock against his stomach, and nuzzle his neck as I squeeze the shaft. Biting his earlobe, I whisper, "You're my sweet slut, and you're using such nice manners today. I think you deserve a reward for being so good."

In one graceful movement, I throw my leg over his broad chest and straddle him, pinning his upper body to the bed. I reach over to grab the hot pink fuzzy handcuffs from our toy stash in the nightstand drawer.

I give him a stern order. "Put your hands above your head, my sweet boy. Don't you dare move them."

"Yes, Mistress. Anything you say," he agrees breathlessly, his eyes shining with worship.

He obediently raises his arms, and I feed the fluffy cuffs through the wrought iron bars of our headboard and secure them snugly to his wrists, immobilizing him. I'm briefly tempted to scoot up and ride his talented tongue until I'm screaming in ecstasy, but the ache in my core tells me I really want to feel his cock inside me. I move back down his body until his shaft is trapped between his body and my wet, swollen pussy.

I glide my pussy along the length of his cock, savoring the delicious friction against my throbbing clit. Throwing my head back, I groan loudly in pleasure. "Fuck, that feels amazing, baby."

I undulate my hips, working myself up into a frenzy as I use Jackson like my own personal sex toy. But as wonderful as this feels, I'm ready to kick things up a notch and really blow his mind. First though, I need to tease him a little and see how he reacts to the idea of watching another man fuck me. I'm curious to see his uncensored reaction.

Leaning forward and bracing myself with one hand splayed on his chest, I dangle my tits enticingly in his face, the dusky pink nipples puckered and just begging to be sucked. I keep them maddeningly just out of range of his eager mouth as I roll and pinch one sensitive peak between my thumb and index finger. Jackson moans helplessly, straining against the cuffs, as I continue to slide my drenched pussy up and down his shaft.

"Tell me something, my sweet, slutty boy," I purr, finally bringing one nipple to his parted lips. He immediately latches on hungrily, sucking it and making me gasp. I let him worship my tits for a minute before cruelly pulling them away. "Have you ever fantasized about watching another man fuck me? Letting some hung stud rail your wife right in front of you?"

It's a risky, bold question, I know. He and I have never seriously discussed bringing another person into our bedroom before. But every time Jackson talked about our various friends exploring the hotwife lifestyle, he always sounded more curious and intrigued than disapproving or turned off.

His eyes widen in shock at my question, but I also see an unmistakable spark of hunger flare in their depths as he breathes out, "Jesus, Marcela. Do you... is that something you want to try?"

I grind my hips down harder against his cock in response. "I'm the one asking the questions here, slut," I remind him sternly, before letting my voice go all breathy and seductive again. "Have you ever imagined watching me get railed by a massive cock?"

"God, yes, I have," Jackson admits with a strangled groan as his face contorts in pleasure. "Someone who will fuck you hard while I watch. I want to see you fall apart on another man's cock, Mistress. Will you do it for me someday, please?"

Holy shit, what? I wasn't expecting him to admit it and then ask me to do it. Searing hot pleasure ripples down my spine at his confession and my entire body lights on fire. This is beyond my wildest dreams, and so insanely hot I can hardly think straight. But I know he and I need to have a discussion about this when his mind isn't totally fogged with lust.

I give my voice a singsong lilt. "Maybe I will, if you keep being such a good boy for me."

There's a hunger written all over his face as I move my hand down and grasp the base of his shaft. I slide it against my pussy lips, teasing the entrance and making us both crazed. He jerks against the handcuffs, flexing his hips upward, and I can tell my sweet slut is desperate to feel my pussy around his cock.

I line up the head of his cock in the perfect spot and sink down on him.

The moisture between my thighs helps him slide inside easily, and I moan at the exquisite pleasure as my pussy molds around him.

He groans loudly once he's balls deep in my pussy. This right here is always my favorite moment. I enjoy it when my slut services me, but I get a bigger sexual thrill from watching him take pleasure.

I rotate my hips slowly, feeling every inch of his cock massaging my inner walls. "If I let you come, are you going to be a good boy and make me breakfast in the morning?"

He lifts his hips, trying to force me to ride him faster. "Yes," he pants. "Anything you want."

Bracing my hands on his chest for leverage, I start to bounce on his cock, angling my hips so he hits that magic spot inside me just right. My body thrums with excitement, and I close my eyes. The only sounds in the room are our combined moans and the squeak of the bed as we surge together. I can feel my orgasm building, and I know that he'll be a good boy and wait for me to come.

As I fuck him hard and fast, I imagine another guy in the room filling my ass. I'm so surprised at the double stuffed fantasy that it tumbles me into my orgasm.

I cry out, "Oh god, I'm coming!" as wave after wave of toe-curling pleasure crashes over me.

My vision swims as I quiver around his cock. My entire body is wired as I slam my pussy down and grind against him, seeking out the last bits of pleasure.

I take a few moments to recover, and when I can think again, I can tell how badly Jackson needs to come. He's still hard inside me, his shaft pulsing with the force of his denied release.

I kiss him slowly as I stroke his cheek, feeling so lucky that I married a man who lets me treat him like a sexual object when I want, and lets me love him tenderly when I don't. "Thank you for your service, my sweet boy."

His cock jumps with excitement as I move my mouth down to suck on the tender skin of his neck. I'm ready for him to fill me with his cum. I start to lazily rock my hips, squeezing my inner muscles around his shaft. His answering groan is music to my ears.

I tease him one final time. "Beg for it, my sweet boy. Beg to fill my pussy."

"Mistress," he gasps, his eyes snapping shut. I can tell by his expression he's on the brink. "Please, please. Let me fill you. Oh, fuck."

He's so sweet when he's begging, but I put him out of his misery and command, "Come for me."

"Fuck, Mistress! Oh shit, fuck yes!" he moans, his cock twitching inside me with the force of his intense orgasm.

I feel his warm cum bathe my insides and I keep rocking, milking his cock for every last drop. Knowing I gave him pleasure makes me feel sexy and powerful.

After he comes down, I free his wrists from the handcuffs and cuddle with him, enjoying the scent of our lovemaking. He wraps his arms around me and he's quiet for a long time. I smile to myself, knowing that the stronger his orgasm is, the longer it takes for his brain to work.

"Mmm, that was amazing as always, baby. You did so good," I praise him, enjoying the blissful afterglow. "Thank you for letting me use you like that. You're such a good boy for me."

Jackson pulls me closer, nuzzling his face into my hair. "I love being your good boy. You really do deserve whatever you want for breakfast."

I giggle and kiss his chest. "I'm a simple girl; bacon, eggs, and toast, please."

"Your wish is my command, Mistress. I love you so much," he murmurs drowsily.

I smile and hug him tighter, breathing in his familiar, comforting scent. "I love you too, baby. More than anything."

I'll wait until morning when we're both fully awake to discuss what he said during sex. It was probably just the heat of the moment, but I'm not going to complain if my husband WANTS me to fuck someone else.

Chapter 2

After a delicious breakfast the next morning, we're snuggled up on the living room sofa watching a TV show. We're relaxing today, and we planned to watch two back-to-back episodes, but to my surprise, he pauses the show after the first one ends, turning to face me with an unreadable expression.

"Is something up, baby?" I ask lightly, trying to keep the sudden unease out of my voice. My mind immediately flashes back to the erotic banter last night, my body warming up at the memory.

Jackson clears his throat, looking oddly nervous. "Um, yeah, actually. We need to talk."

Pasting on what I hope is a reassuring smile, I squeeze his knee. "What's on your mind, love?"

He takes my hand, threading our fingers together. I rub my thumb soothingly over his skin, trying to ease both our nerves as I wonder if this is it—the moment of truth. Is he about to admit that he was caught up in the heat of the moment and he doesn't want me to be a hotwife, or is he going to confess he really does? Am I going to be disappointed if he doesn't?

Jackson studies our entwined hands and the seconds tick by in silence. Finally, I can't take it anymore. I gently remove my hand from his and reach up to cup his cheek, forcing him to meet my eyes. "Jackson, look at me."

His eyes blaze with an intensity that surprises me, and he finally speaks.

"I want to watch another man fuck you, but not just anyone," he admits.

Wow. Okay. I'm already nodding because it's an easy request. I don't want it to be just anyone either. If I'm going to fuck someone else, I want it to be mind-blowingly hot and memorable. And if I'm being honest, I'd like someone with a big cock. Not that Jackson is small by any means, but I've always been curious what it would feel like to be split open on a really massive dick, you know?

Mentally shaking myself out of my X-rated musings, I refocus on my husband, who is watching me closely. "I want it to be a guy who can give you what I can't," he continues urgently. "What I'm not giving you."

Wait, what's that supposed to mean? Does he think I'm not satisfied with our amazing sex life and he's not enough for me? The thought makes me feel uneasy.

"Baby, no. You make me happier than I ever thought possible," I rush to reassure him, stroking his stubbled cheek. "I don't need anything or anyone else."

To my relief, Jackson chuckles, his eyes crinkling at the corners. "I know that, sweetheart. Believe me, I do." He leans in to kiss me softly before saying sheepishly, "I didn't phrase that very well."

As if to prove his point, he takes my hand and places it on his denim-clad crotch. I can feel that his cock is already semi-erect and growing harder by the second. Holy fuck.

He grins at me. "That's not what I meant. What I was trying to say is... I've been fantasizing about watching someone dominant absolutely wreck you and do all the things to you that I'm not confident enough to do myself. I want to see the blissed-out, totally fucked look on your beautiful face when he's railing you and making you come so hard you scream. I just...fuck, I want to be there experiencing it with you as you're getting your mind blown by a real Dom guy."

I gape at him, completely speechless. He's been fantasizing about this? Like, specific, detailed fantasies of another man dominating the fuck out of me while he watches? Jesus Christ. A pleasurable shock zings through my body like an electric current, making my nerve endings sizzle and my pussy flood with moisture. My clit throbs in time with my racing pulse as I picture it—Jackson stroking his cock as he sits in a chair a few feet away, watching me get pounded into oblivion by a dominant stranger. The forbidden image is so searingly erotic that my brain shorts out for a minute, lost to the fantasy.

When I finally regain the power of speech, my voice trembles with need. "You've really been fantasizing about this?"

He nods, swallowing hard, and I can see a telltale flush creeping up his neck above the collar of his t-shirt. He's blushing. It's adorable and sexy as hell.

Emboldened, I start to slowly rub his stiffening cock through his jeans, feeling it twitch and swell. He groans low in his throat, hips shifting restlessly as I give him a firm squeeze. "Tell me, baby...have you been stroking yourself while imagining another man dominating me? Picturing him wrecking my pussy with his enormous cock until I'm a writhing, screaming mess? Is that what gets you off these days?"

"Yes," he rasps. "Sometimes when I'm watching porn, I imagine it's you in the video, practically cross-eyed with pleasure. I can't help it."

Fuck me, this is so deliciously dirty and unexpected. Who knew my sweet, submissive husband had such a filthy, voyeuristic side? The revelation makes desire swirl in my lower belly. "Mmm, you naughty boy. Did you stroke your cock faster when the man in the video started groaning as he got close? Did you imagine him blowing his big load all over me while you watched?" I ask breathlessly, rubbing him harder through his jeans.

Jackson's hands clench into fists at his sides and he squeezes his eyes shut, clearly fighting for control. His hips buck up into my touch and he moans, "Yes, Mistress. I did."

I click my tongue in mock disapproval even as my pussy grows increasingly wet. "Eyes open. Look at me when you're confessing your dirty secrets,"

He obeys instantly, staring up at me. "Good boy. Now, why the hell didn't you tell me about this sexy fantasy of yours sooner, hmm?"

Jackson shrugs helplessly, looking flustered. "I don't know. I guess it was just a private fantasy at first. I didn't think you'd actually want to do it for real."

My heart melts a little at his sweetness, even as my body screams at me to strip him naked and ride him until we both pass out. But first, we need to get a few things straight. Letting go of his straining erection, I put my hand under his chin instead, tilting his face up to mine and forcing him to maintain eye contact. I use my normal, everyday voice so he understands this is just me, his wife, talking to him, not his Mistress.

"Baby, listen to me. I would absolutely love to fulfill this fantasy for you. For us. But only if you're really, truly sure you want it too," I say seriously, holding his gaze. "I don't need other men to be satisfied, physically or emotionally. What you and I have fulfills me. You're more than enough for me, always. I need you to know that."

He smiles at me tenderly, his eyes going soft and warm. "I do know that, Marcela. I promise. You're all I need too. I want this because the thought of sharing you, of watching you come undone with another man, is a huge fucking turn-on for me. But only because I know at the end of the day, your heart belongs to me. I'm secure in that. In us."

If I wasn't ready to jump him before, I sure as hell am now. This man! Overwhelmed with love and passion, I surge forward and crash my lips to his in a bruising kiss, moaning into his mouth as I straddle his lap. He kisses me back just as fiercely, his strong arms wrapping around my waist and hauling me closer. We make out for several minutes until we're both panting.

Breaking away with a gasp, I roll my hips against the rigid line of his cock, seeking friction. "Well, in that case...start looking for a well-hung guy to fuck your wife, baby," I grin wickedly. "Because I'm all in."

Jackson grasps my gyrating hips, holding me in place. "Fuck yes," he groans. "Thank you, Mistress."

I kiss him one last time before reluctantly climbing off his lap on shaky legs. I'm tempted to pull his cock out and fuck him right now, but I resist... barely.

Smirking at his dazed, lust-drunk expression, I press one finger to his kiss-swollen lips in a shushing gesture as he opens his mouth to protest the loss of contact. "That's all you get until you find a sexy Dom to fuck your wife while you watch," I tease, tracing the seam of his lips. He nips at my finger, eyes dancing with mischief, and I tap his nose in reproach. "Be a good boy. Just think about how incredible it'll feel when I fuck you after you watch me get absolutely wrecked by a big, thick cock. The wait will be more than worth it, trust me."

Jackson mutters something that sounds suspiciously like, "Evil, cock-teasing succubus," under his breath, but wisely keeps any other complaints to himself. I know I have him exactly where I want him—horny as hell and willing to do anything to get some relief.

"So, you have your orders. Find me a stud to play with, and I'll give you the ride of your life afterwards. Now I'm going to get some water for the next episode."

I sashay out of the room with an extra sway to my hips, grinning like the cat that caught the canary. I have a feeling my kinky husband will have found the perfect guy to dom the hell out of me by this time next week.

This is going to be fun.

CHAPTER 3

I was wrong. He found someone the next day.

I work from home as a transcriptionist and when I take my first break on Monday, there's a text waiting for me.

Jackson

I got you a guy.

My body tingles from a zing of pleasure and my nipples harden.

Marcela

Oh? That was fast.

Grabbing a glass of water, some string cheese, and grapes, I settle onto the sofa. This conversation deserves my full attention. I smile and take a sip of water as I see the chat bubbles pop up as my husband is replying.

Jackson

I actually found three guys. You get your pick, or you can have them all at once.

His words make me suck in my breath, which turns into a coughing fit as I try to swallow the water down the wrong pipe. Holy fuck... Yes, please! I didn't even contemplate more than one man as an option. I mean, I've got three holes... I don't even know what to say, so I type without thinking.

Marcela

Do I want that many at once?

Jackson

I think you do.

Well, hell, if he wants me to have three cocks…

Marcela

You're right. I do. Who are they?

Jackson types out the details while I eat my snack. Victor, one of his work buddies, has always thought I was super hot. When Jackson joked with Victor about fucking me to see if he'd really want to do it, Victor said he had two friends he could bring along to show me a really good time. I guess the guys have done this before.

Fuck, that's slutty, and so damn hot. I type to my husband and tell him to set it up.

I can barely pay attention to work after that as I daydream about fucking multiple men. I love being domme for my husband, but my submissive side doesn't get to play much. This experience isn't just about fucking another man; the idea that I can really become a submissive slut is the best part.

Jackson keeps texting me and we discuss everything. He's checking with his coworker to find out when they're all free. The plan is to have them come over to our house, but after I agree to it, I almost wish we were going somewhere else. My filthy side wants to embrace the naughtiness of what we're doing and I'm not sure our house is going to make me feel like we're doing something illicit.

After lunch, I give up pretending I'm working. I try on some sexy lingerie, debating what to wear. I send my husband a photo of myself from the neck down. I'm topless with a sexy garter belt and lace black thong, and tell him to share it with the guys so they can see what they're getting. Now that I've embraced the plan to be a hotwife, I'm so turned on it's crazy.

As I put away the lingerie tossed in a pile on the bed, Jackson sends me another text.

Jackson

> They just told me they're free tonight. Want to fuck them tonight?

I'm so shocked, I laugh out loud and dial his number immediately. As soon as I hear his voice, an idea comes to me. I don't care that I sound like a total slut when I tell him, "I want it to be at a cheap motel. Make it happen and text me the address and time. I'll meet you there."

My sweet, submissive husband confirms my request. "I'll have the room ready."

I hang up the phone and stare at the wall as my body buzzes. I guess I'm getting all my holes stuffed tonight in a cheap motel so I can feel extra dirty and used.

The idea thrills me to no end, but I'm suddenly overcome by the magnitude of this experience. Am I really doing this? I know it's something I want, but it still feels unreal. My head spins as I change into my sluttiest outfit. The black skirt I pick out is tight and barely covers my ass, and my blouse is a low cut V-neck that I'm practically popping out of. I forgo a bra and I can tell my nipples will pop against the fabric of my shirt. The last item of clothing is a sexy black thong. I decide to wear my long brown hair in a ponytail so it doesn't get caught on all the extra body parts.

I apply minimal makeup, knowing it will be a mess by the end of the night. Yep, I'm a practical gal. I slip on my four-inch fuck-me heels and practice walking in them for a few minutes. Hopefully, I won't be wearing them for very long.

I imagine showing up and stripping in the hotel room in front of everyone, and I shiver from longing. If someone had told me two days ago that I'd be fucking multiple guys tonight, I wouldn't have believed them.

Yeah, I'm really doing this. I'm about to become a hotwife.

Right before I leave, I toss a bottle of lube into my purse. I'm not sure if anyone will want to use my ass, but I'm going to be prepared. There's a certain thrill from knowing I'm not meeting Jackson at a fancy hotel for a romantic rendezvous. Nope, I'm going to a seedy motel where he and I are renting a room for the sole purpose of a hard pussy pounding. The anticipation is exhilarating. I just hope I can relax enough to lose my inhibitions. What if fucking people I don't know is awkward?

By the time I get there, I'm shaking with arousal and nervousness. I park my car, grab my purse, and hurry to the room, eager to get fucked.

I knock on the door, and Jackson opens it with a grin. "Hi."

"Hi." I smile back at him and he steps aside to let me in. We arranged for the guys to arrive after me, so we're alone right now. As the door closes, I scan the room, and it's exactly as I expected: threadbare carpet and mismatched furniture, with an air conditioner unit rattling from the corner. It's perfect for the occasion.

Jackson touches my ass, and I glance over my shoulder and purr at him, "Like what you see?"

"Oh yeah," he laughs, and when I turn towards him, his gaze fixes on my chest.

My nipples harden and I almost giggle as I say, "My eyes are up here, baby."

He's vibrating with desire when he looks up, and I get a nice thrill from knowing he's turned on as much as I am. I press my body against his, sliding my arms around his neck and pulling him down for a kiss. When our lips touch, it's all fire and passion. He's so familiar and comforting, yet exciting at the same time.

When we come up for air, his eyes are clouded with lust. I give him a teasing pat on the butt and say, "Okay, hands off the merchandise. Save your energy for the main event."

There's a large mirror on the wall above a small dresser, and I notice my cheeks are extra pink and my eyes sparkle. Yeah, I'm a horny slut. I set my purse on the dresser and fish out the lube before looking at Jackson with a smirk. "Should I be naked when they get here?"

He doesn't have time to answer because there's a sharp rap on the door. My stomach jumps from excitement. My first foray into being a hotwife is about to begin.

Jackson rushes to the door and opens it to reveal three muscular guys. I swear, as soon as the men enter the room, my pussy grows even wetter. Oh my god, I'm getting dicked down in a seedy motel room by these gorgeous men?

Two of the men are white, one with blonde hair and the other bald, and the third guy is Black with dark hair. They're all extremely good looking and athletic. They're casually dressed in jeans and t-shirts, and I can already see impressive bulges underneath the denim.

Jackson clears his throat to get my attention. "Marcela, this is Victor, Daniel, and Shawn."

I quickly try to memorize their names. Victor is the blonde guy, Daniel is bald, and Shawn is Black.

All of them greet me with friendly waves and smiles, and I relax as I return the greeting. "Nice to meet you."

Victor seems to be the leader of the group, and he takes charge. He moves in close and cups my jaw, tipping my face up. My pulse races as I stare into his eyes.

"This isn't how I normally fuck other people's wives, so I need to hear you say you want it."

The fact that he's worried about consent makes my panties even wetter, and my voice is breathy. "I want all of you to fuck me."

He studies me, and apparently he's satisfied with my answer. A slow, devilish smile curves his lips. "Good to know. We're going to have fun toying with you."

His words and tone of voice immediately start making me feel submissive, and I can already tell this is going to be fabulous. It's been so long since I've felt the delicious mindlessness of being someone's fucktoy, and I'm ready to embrace my sluttiest side.

He takes my hand and leads me to the center of the room. My chest is heaving and I'm having a difficult time catching my breath as his fingers ghost down my throat. "One last detail to work out. Your husband wants us to dominate you and turn you into a wet puddle. What do you want?"

A deep longing grips me, and I almost forget to breathe. Holy hell, I'm already a wet puddle. Mission accomplished.

When I realize they're all staring at me and waiting for my answer, I say in a rush, "I want that. Dominate me. Treat me like a dirty slut who's only here to satisfy all of you." The longer I talk, the faster the words spill out, coming from deep within me. "Break me down until I can't think. Just fuck me senseless, please. I'll do whatever you want."

Victor shares a look with his friends. "In that case, slut, get on your knees and open your mouth."

I tremble with excitement as I awkwardly kneel next to the bed. My damn high heels are already getting in the way, but the struggle just makes me feel dirtier. Looking up at them ready to use me and knowing they could fuck my mouth all night and I wouldn't complain is the final piece that snaps me into my most submissive self. I'm completely ready to be used.

Jackson sits in a chair facing the bed, and the other guys remove their shirts. My gaze lands on their taut stomachs and chiseled chests. My body buzzes as I imagine how their skin is going to feel against mine. It's been over ten years since I've intimately touched a man other than Jackson, and I'm curious to explore the differences between the men.

My heart flutters when I hear a zipper lowering right behind me, and my scalp prickles as my ponytail is taken by a fist and my head is pulled back. I blink to clear my vision and focus. It's Daniel. He's leaning over me, his expression fierce.

"Do you know what a mouth is for, slut?"

I manage to murmur, "For sucking cocks."

"Show me, whore," he demands.

It's so hot to hear a stranger call me degrading names like that. He moves in front of me and guides his cock to my mouth. I shudder with pleasure as I lick the underside of his shaft.

Daniel's hands wrap around my head, and the pressure he applies intensifies when I part my lips to take him into my mouth. His steel rod slides past my lips and I curl my tongue around the tip before opening wider. His cock is bigger than my husband's and I daydream of how it will feel inside my pussy as I suck on him, swirling my tongue across his velvety skin.

I feel another man behind me and I hear the sounds of a zipper and the rustling of fabric. My heart races with excitement.

Daniel's grip on my head tightens as he thrusts deeper into my mouth. I can taste his pre-cum, and it makes me even more eager to please him. I moan around his cock, and the vibrations make him groan in pleasure.

Victor interrupts. "Let's put the slut on the bed. I need to use a hole."

Oh, wow. Daniel pulls out of my mouth and helps me to my feet. I kick off my heels in relief, and suddenly three pairs of hands are all over me, tugging and pulling at my clothes. It's like a whirlwind, and before I can blink, I'm standing naked while all eyes are on me. I feel a rush of vulnerability and I want to hide my tits behind my hands, but I force myself to stand tall and let the men examine me.

Victor takes charge again and pushes me onto the bed. "Get on your hands and knees."

I scramble to obey and position myself at an angle that gives Jackson a side view of the action. Daniel stands in front of me while I eagerly suck on him. I wasn't done with my treat.

Victor climbs on the bed behind me and grabs my hips, and his hard cock presses against my ass. I tremble with desire as he rubs the tip of his cock, poking at my asshole, teasing me. Shit, should I tell him to get the lube? Not that I really can, since my mouth is busy.

When the tip of his cock probes the entrance of my pussy, I relax—yeah, okay, that hole is nice and wet for him. He thrusts forward, filling me in one swift motion. I cry out around Daniel's cock as Victor starts to fuck me hard and fast.

Ooooh, he's not wasting time. I throw myself into the blow job as delight ripples through me from Victor's hard thrusts. I can feel myself getting wetter as the bliss swirls in my core. At this rate, I'm going to come quickly. Victor's cock is hitting all the right spots in my pussy, and the room spins from the pleasure.

I start to move my hips in rhythm with Victor, meeting him thrust for thrust. I can hear the sound of our bodies slapping together and it's so fucking hot.

Shawn moves in front of me, his cock already hard and ready. He grabs my chin and pulls me away from Daniel's cock. "It's my turn."

I eagerly open my mouth. He's bigger than Daniel, and it takes me a moment to adjust to his size as he slides in. I'm determined to please him, and I suck and lick his cock with abandon.

Victor is still fucking me hard, and I can feel myself getting closer and closer to my orgasm. Every time I moan around Shawn's cock, it makes him inhale from pleasure. Being used in two holes at once pings the part of my brain that loves being a fucktoy. I'm on cloud nine, and knowing Jackson is watching makes it so much better.

When Victor reaches underneath me to rub my clit while he fucks me, the sensation shoots me over the edge. My body goes rigid, and I come apart as I shake with pleasure. When my pussy seizes around Victor's cock, he hisses and pulls out before he comes.

My head is whirling from delight when Shawn pulls out of my mouth and lies down on the bed. I'm woozy from the pleasure of my orgasm as Victor and Daniel lift me up and set me down on Shawn's cock. Being moved around like a sex toy is so damn hot.

I moan loudly as I sink down on Shawn's shaft, his thick cock stretching me. His hands wrap around my waist and he thrusts up into me. Holy hell, he feels amazing. It's like he's pinging every nerve ending inside me and I mewl out little peeps of delight.

"Fuck her harder," Victor demands, and Shawn complies without hesitation. His hands tighten on my sides as he forces me to move with him and grind against the base of his cock. It's borderline painful, but it's a glorious pleasure. My husband picked some fabulous guys.

Daniel comes up behind me. "Get ready for some serious ass pounding."

He presses on my shoulder and I lean forward. Mmm, yes, please. I gasp as Daniel applies the lube to my ass, working it in with his finger before his cock slides into my ass. Ooooh, god. I've never had two cocks at once, and I moan as the pleasure threatens to overwhelm me.

Shawn grunts as he thrusts deeper into me, and a tingling sensation zips through me, straight to my pussy. How did I not do this in college when I was going through my slut phase and experimenting? It's sensory overload and I've never felt as full as I do right now.

"You're so fucking tight," Shawn growls, and Daniel agrees. "God, she is. I could fuck this ass all night long."

Out of the corner of my eye, I can see Jackson watching everything. He's stroking his cock over his jeans with a rapt expression on his face. Thank god he's enjoying this.

Victor kneels next to me, moving his cock towards my face. A delicious ache between my legs makes me almost smile. Mmm, yes... all holes will be stuffed. I open my mouth eagerly as he slides in.

My body is on fire and I'm lost in a haze of pleasure. This might be heaven right here—assuming it's filled with massive cocks. My heaven would be.

I moan and writhe with pleasure between the men as they fuck me. I'm their sex toy to use, just a bunch of holes...and I love it. Every part of me zings with euphoria and I feel like I'm going to explode as I'm barreling towards another orgasm. This one is going to be intense.

Victor grips my hair, pulling me closer to him as he thrusts into my mouth. I can feel his cock hitting the back of my throat, and I gag slightly, but I don't care. I want to please him and make him come as hard as his friends are about to make me.

Daniel's fingers dig into my hips as he fucks me harder, his cock hitting that perfect spot inside me. I moan around Victor's cock, my body shaking with pleasure.

Shawn's hands are on my breasts, squeezing and pinching my nipples as every thrust into my ass forces me down harder onto his cock. I'm lost in the moment, my body being used and pleasured by three men at once. It's everything I've ever fantasized about, and it's even better than I imagined.

Victor suddenly pulls out of my mouth, his cock glistening with my saliva. He strokes his cock, aiming the tip towards my face. Oh god, is he going to give me a facial?

When Shawn's cock hits a particularly pleasurable spot, I gasp and open my mouth. Victor rubs the tip across my lips. I try to lick on him and suck on the head of his cock, but he pulls it away.

I'm spiraling closer and closer to my orgasm, and I cry out as my body shudders, my pussy contracting around Shawn's cock as he pounds into me.

Daniel spanks me and the pain adds to my pleasure and tips me over the edge. I scream out with my orgasm and Daniel growls, "That's it, come for us. Such a dirty slut, letting all of us fuck you at the same time."

As I ride out the waves of my orgasm, Victor pushes his cock deep into my mouth. I gag on his cock again, but he doesn't pull out. Instead, he holds me in place, making me drool around his shaft as he fucks my mouth. Somehow, he knows exactly how much I can take. It's the perfect roughness, and I love it.

As my orgasm subsides, I'm left breathless and weak, but the guys aren't done with me yet. Daniel speeds up his thrusts into my ass, and the pleasure builds. There's no way I'm not going to want to do this again—maybe next time I can have a cock in each hand as well. Five at once... the ultimate slut.

Since I can think a little easier now, I try to focus on my husband and make sure he's still okay. He looks dazed, like his mind is fuzzy, but I can tell he's entranced by the scene. He probably didn't know how big of a slut he married. After this experience, I'm ready to take on an entire sports team.

When Jackson realizes I'm looking at him, he smiles at me and continues stroking his cock through his pants. If my mouth wasn't full of cock, I'd blow him a kiss.

I'm brought back to what's happening to me when Shawn sucks on a nipple. As he massages my other breast, a zing of pleasure heads straight to my clit. Having both guys in me, someone sucking on a tit, and a cock in my mouth is too much.

I explode.

The orgasm that rolls through my body is unlike any I've ever experienced before. My legs shake, and I'm overcome with waves of pleasure as I cry out. I'm suddenly in a place where I can feel everything all at once and my vision blurs from euphoria.

Victor pulls out of my mouth, but Daniel and Shawn keep going, driving me to another peak as my mind splinters from pleasure. Stars burst behind my eyelids as my orgasm seems to go on and on. A dark thrill winds its way through me and I know I'm just a fucktoy for them to use all they want. I'd give them anything. I don't know how much more I can take, but I know I don't want it to end.

I lose track of how many times I come. My mind is reeling, and my body is completely spent. I feel like I'm floating on a cloud, and I have a hard time focusing as they continue to use me.

Eventually, it's as if time speeds up, and everything happens at once. Daniel groans a moment before he blows his load in my ass. I feel his cum filling me, and the sensation is exquisite. I clench around Shawn's cock in my pussy and he hisses as I milk his cock for all he's worth. Shawn's entire body spasms as he comes deep inside me. Ropes of sticky cum coat my inner walls, and I imagine it gushing out of me when he pulls out. I've been filled in both holes, and I look around for Victor. Where did he go?

He's standing next to the bed, stroking his cock, and after Daniel pulls out of my ass, Victor pushes me off of Shawn and rolls me onto my back.

I've barely come down from the last orgasm before my pussy is being filled with Victor's cock. Oh god!

"You still like it hard, right?" Victor asks.

I nod and brace myself for his relentless pace as Victor pounds away at my pussy. Within moments, I can already feel another orgasm building. Can someone pass out from bliss?

I don't have time to think about it too much as Shawn climbs onto the bed and kneels by my head. He grabs my hand and wraps it around his shaft, and he moans as I stroke him. I love the way he's taking control and using me for his own pleasure.

Shawn's cock is wet from my juices, and it pulses in my hand as he gets closer to another release. I run my thumb over the head of his shaft and it's like flipping a switch. He shudders and explodes, aiming for my tits. Three shots of cum hit me.

I close my eyes and concentrate on the sensations. When Victor brings a hand down to my clit and brushes circles around it, I detonate. I cry out, my body writhing in ecstasy as the orgasm pulses through me.

I'm still trembling and twitching as the last drops of come drip down onto my chest. Victor groans and jerks several times. I can feel his warm cum filling me up and mixing with Shawn's previous load.

When Victor rolls off of me, I assume everyone is done with me, but Daniel walks out of the bathroom and he's hard again. He pulls me to the edge of the bed so my head is hanging off and he guides his cock into my mouth. I can tell he cleaned up in the bathroom as his shaft sinks into my throat.

He leans over me, bracing his hands on the bed while he uses my throat as his fleshlight. I've never been treated this way, and it's absolutely amazing. Someone at the other end of the bed spreads my legs and starts rubbing the cum dripping out of me around my clit. They aren't finger fucking me, they're just playing with the combined wetness between my legs. It's almost dirtier this way, and I moan around Daniel's cock.

The vibration of my moan sets Daniel off and he blows his load deep in my throat. When he pulls out, cum and saliva smear across my cheek and I almost giggle. I'm sure I look wrecked.

I glance down at the guy playing with my pussy and get a shock when it's Jackson. Oh fuck. My husband is playing with the cum in my pussy. When he sees me look at him, he smiles.

"You're so wet."

I'm too mentally fucked to do anything but moan in pleasure as he continues to swirl his fingers around my clit. My husband briefly stops playing with my pussy to pull me all the way back up onto the bed, but then he resumes his fingering as he talks to the guys. I close my eyes and I'm vaguely aware of the men getting dressed.

I can barely move a muscle, but I also feel more satisfied than I ever have in my life. I let out a contented sigh as the men gather up their things and leave with a collective, "Thank you."

The door shuts and I'm alone with my husband. I muster the energy to pat the bed next to me.

"Take your clothes off and come cuddle, baby."

I'm not sure what I have the energy for, but I desperately need contact with him. I need to feel him inside me and hear him say that he still loves me after watching me be such a filthy slut.

Jackson gets undressed and when he's next to me, I can't help but chuckle.

He raises his eyebrows. "What's funny?"

I grab his still-hard cock. "This. You still want me."

He smiles. "I'll never stop wanting you, not in a million years. How do you feel?"

My whole body aches in a pleasant way, and I don't want him worrying about that. This is now his time. I kiss his nose and squeeze his cock. "I'm sore in all the right ways, and I really, really love you."

His grin is so bright it warms my insides. His fingers trail up my arm and he moves them to my nipple, tweaking it. "I really, really love you, too. It was so hot, watching you get dominated."

When he massages the sticky cum into my breasts, I realize he's staring at his hands. He's definitely fascinated with the fluid. I can't blame him for it since I enjoy it as well. I moan as his hand returns to my pussy and his finger runs between my folds.

I hum with pleasure and murmur softly, "So you liked that?"

He chuckles. "More than I expected."

My pussy is getting too sensitive, and I give him a gentle order. "Stop toying with me and get your cock inside me. I need you."

He hesitates. "You're sure? I could wait. You've been through a lot."

My heart warms from how sweet he is. I can see how desperately he wants me, and I bet he'd wait if I asked him to.

"I want you, baby."

I open my arms to him and he covers my body with his. He's gentle as his cock fills me with one stroke, and I moan as he bottoms out. It feels different. I'm stuffed full of the other guys' cum, but Jackson's cock feels new. I need this, this connection with the love of my life after fucking other men.

"You feel so good," he murmurs against my shoulder as he slowly fucks me.

When he tries to kiss me, I hold his cheek to stop him. "You sure you want to kiss your wife after she sucked on two cocks?"

His nostrils flare, and I know I've turned him on with the dirty talk. His voice is gruff when he says, "That makes me want to kiss you even more."

The desperation in his voice is thrilling. I'm a slut, and it's sexy to be his slut. His lips descend to mine, and we kiss deeply, our tongues twining as we rock together. I love the way he makes me feel. It's like electricity crackling between us, and I can't get enough. The steady rhythm of his cock makes me sigh. I let go and float along, enjoying the moment. He's worshiping my body with his hands and cock, and it's lovely to feel like I've come home. He's mine and I'm his, and no one can ever take that away from us.

When his breath quickens and his moans get louder, I whisper to him. "You can fuck me harder. I need you to come."

Jackson kisses me and I arch my hips so he can fuck me deeper as his thrusting grows more urgent. He grasps my hips tightly with both hands and I wonder if there'll be bruises tomorrow. He's my gentle giant, so for him to be using such force means he's consumed with desire.

I can tell he's getting close, so I give him the command. "Come for me. Give me everything."

That's the breaking point. He comes hard.

His muscles strain and his hips buck. I'm wrapped around him, my fingers digging into his shoulders, and I can feel when his control slips and he surrenders to his release. He comes hard, crying out as he buries his face in my neck. I cling to him as he spills his seed inside me. I never want to let go.

His climax triggers a surprise orgasm for me, and I cry out as we both ride the waves of bliss. My mind blanks from pleasure and I'm not sure how long we stay locked together.

When my brain finally starts working, his face is still buried in my neck and his heavy breaths tickle my skin. I can't stop smiling. My heart swells as I run my hands along his back.

He lifts his head to give me a questioning look. "Is it bad that I want to do this again someday?"

I laugh as I push him off of me. "Maybe someday, if my good boy begs enough, I might let him watch other men fuck me again."

He just grins and starts licking the cum off my breasts. I shiver as he lavishes attention on my nipples. Yeah, he's definitely my good boy... but more importantly, a whole new world of opportunities has opened up for our marriage. If he wants to watch a train of guys dominate me and fuck me, I'm open to the idea.

Being a hotwife might just be the best thing that's happened for our marriage.

My friends are going to think this is hilarious. I can't wait for the next poker night to tell them.

The End

June Hotwife

Hotwife of the Month Book 6

Lacey Cross

CHAPTER 1

I smile and wave to our friends as we leave the monthly get-together at Marcela's house. It was a great night, with laughter and chatter from the girls' night upstairs while the guys played poker downstairs. My husband Mark's hand rests lightly on the small of my back as we make our way to our sensible family sedan parked at the curb.

As our friends Ana and Max climb into their car ahead of us, Ana turns back and gives me a wave, her eyes sparkling with mischief. I grin back at her, my mind still reeling from her earlier confession. Sweet, shy Ana is apparently a hotwife now. Her husband watched her with another guy. The very idea sparks a forbidden thrill within me.

Juliet saunters over to me, her hips swaying in her form-fitting dress. She leans in close, her spicy perfume enveloping me as she stage-whispers in my ear, "Call me tomorrow. I've got some tea to spill that I think you'll find verrry interesting."

She pulls back with a wicked grin, giving me an exaggerated wink before flouncing off to her sleek convertible where her husband is waiting. I chuckle and shake my head as I watch her go, wondering what salacious gossip she's eager to share. With Juliet, it could be anything from a celebrity sighting at her favorite spa to a new sex position she swears will "change your life, honey."

As Mark and I buckle up and pull away from the curb, anticipation flickers in my gut. I know it's silly, but a part of me is hoping my husband will take advantage of our precious few minutes left of being kid-free and ravish me in the back seat like he used to when we were first dating. But the rational side of my brain knows that's unlikely. After a long week of juggling deadlines at my marketing firm, his full-time job, and getting our 4-year-old twins to and from preschool, we're both usually wiped out by the weekend.

The drive home is quiet, and I steal a glance at Mark's profile in the dim glow of the dashboard lights. Even after eight years of marriage, my husband is still sexy to me and I find him incredibly handsome. But lately, I've started to wonder if he still sees me as the vibrant, passionate woman he fell in love with or just the mother of his children and manager of our hectic household.

When we finally get home, I pay the babysitter as Mark heads upstairs. I lock up and check on the kids, and by the time I slip into our bedroom, Mark is already sprawled on his back in bed, one arm flung over his eyes. He's down to his boxers, his toned chest and arms on display. I appreciate how sexy he is as I undress.

"Did you have fun tonight?" he mumbles sleepily, not moving his arm.

"Mmm hmm. It's always fun to visit with the girls." I shimmy out of my dress and kick off my shoes, sighing in relief as I wiggle my newly freed toes.

Mark makes a vaguely affirmative noise, already half asleep. I want to bring up Ana's hotwifing bombshell, if only to gauge his reaction. But suddenly, I'm too tired to get into it. My wine buzz is wearing off, replaced by a bone-deep fatigue and the start of a dull headache throbbing at my temples.

Instead, I finish my nighttime routine in silence, washing the traces of makeup from my face and brushing my teeth before crawling into bed beside Mark. He's fully out now, his breathing deep and even. I curl up on my side facing away from him, trying to ignore the pang of loneliness that lances through my chest.

As I lie there in the dark, my mind drifts back to Ana's revelation. What would it be like to be with another man after all these years with Mark? To feel that electric thrill and experience the heady rush of being wanted, craved, by someone new. The forbidden fantasy sends little sparks of heat through my body.

But that's not my life. All I have this week is an endless slog of work, kids, chores, rinse and repeat. Tomorrow, I'll call Juliet and get the gossip. Maybe it will be the diversion I need. And who knows? Ana could be onto something with this whole hotwifing thing. The idea is crazy, but also...intriguing. Not that I'd ever get the chance, but it might be fun to live vicariously through Ana for a bit. To experience that thrill, even secondhand.

My last thought before I drift off is that I hope Juliet's gossip is juicy enough to get me through another monotonous week. I could use something to look forward to for a change.

CHAPTER 2

The next morning, I'm jolted awake by the sound of my phone buzzing insistently on the nightstand. I groan and grope for it blindly, squinting at the screen through bleary eyes. It's Juliet. Of course. She's never been one to let the suspense build.

I glance over at Mark's side of the bed, but he's already up and out for his Sunday morning run. Probably for the best, since I can talk freely and get the scoop. I answer the phone and try to stifle my yawn.

"Morning, Jules. I'm assuming this is about that gossip you promised?"

"Oh honey, you have no idea," Juliet trills, sounding far too chipper for this ungodly hour. "Are you sitting down? Because trust me, you'll need to be."

I roll my eyes even though she can't see me. "I'm still in bed, so yeah, I'm good. Hit me."

"Okay, so you know our favorite little sanctimonious Debra? Well, apparently she's started a secret blog all about—get this—the 'dangers of open marriages and the hotwife trend.'" Juliet practically cackles with glee. "I guess she's appointed herself the morality police of our friend group."

I sit up straighter, suddenly wide awake. Debra is in our larger circle of friends because her husband went to college with our husbands, but she's been slut shaming our friends for becoming hotwives. "Wait, what? How did you even find out about this?"

"Oh, I have my ways," Juliet says cryptically. "Anyway, you'll never believe the shade she's throwing. Listen to this passage."

Juliet clears her throat dramatically. "'In today's depraved society, it seems that the sanctity of marriage is under constant attack. Everywhere I look, I see once-faithful wives eagerly opening their legs—and their holes—to any man who so much as glances their way. It's a tragic epidemic of sluts gone wild, leaving a trail of broken vows in their wake.'"

"Wow," I breathe, torn between shock and the sudden, wild urge to laugh. "She actually wrote that? And published it online for anyone to see?"

"Oh, it gets better," Juliet assures me. "'I weep for the husbands who are forced to witness their wives' wanton displays of lust and selfish disregard for their marital oaths. How can these women claim to be good wives while allowing their most sacred parts to be defiled night after night?'"

A snort escapes me. Shit, I wish I was so lucky to be getting all of that. I get the giggles, and soon, Juliet and I are both howling with laughter, gasping for breath. "Jesus Christ," I wheeze, wiping tears from my eyes. "'Sacred parts,' really?"

"Right?" Juliet giggles. "I mean, I'm all for Marilyn and Ana getting their freak on, but 'defiled' is a bit much."

"Seriously. If anything, they're being 'defiled' by their own husbands, just like the rest of us. Debra needs to get off her high horse and take the stick out of her ass."

"Ugh, can you imagine how boring missionary must be with Vincent?" Juliet makes a gagging noise. "No wonder she's so uptight."

"Poor thing," I say, my voice dripping with mock sympathy. "She's probably just jealous that she's not getting any of her sacred parts defiled by another man. Lord knows I am."

The words slip out before I can stop them, hanging in the air like a naughty confession. Juliet goes quiet for a moment, and I hold my breath, wondering if I've said too much.

"Wait a minute," she says slowly, her voice taking on a conspiratorial tone. "Would you actually...?"

Heat rushes to my cheeks, and I'm suddenly grateful she can't see me. "What? No! I mean...I don't know. It's crazy, right? I could never actually go through with it."

"Hmm." Juliet sounds thoughtful. "The way you were looking at Ana last night, I thought you were considering taking a page from her playbook."

I'm at a loss for words. Was I that obvious? "I was just...curious, that's all. It's not every day you find out your friend is sleeping around with her husband's blessing."

Juliet giggles. "Hey, no judgment here. Honestly, I'd go for it if Arthur wanted to share me. There's something kinda hot about the whole thing, right?"

I'm saved from having to answer by the sound of a cough at the doorway. Mark is leaning against the doorframe, his running shorts slung low on his hips and a thin sheen of sweat glistening on his bare chest. He looks good enough to eat, and guilt stabs at me for the impure thoughts swirling in my head. Shit, how much did he hear?

I smile at him as I talk to Juliet. "Hey, Mark's back from his run. I gotta go. Talk later?"

"Keep me posted on any developments!"

I end the call and flop back against the pillows and try to play it cool. "Hey there, eavesdropper. Enjoy your run?"

Mark grins and pushes off the doorframe, sauntering over to the bed. "It was all right. Not as exciting as the conversation you were just having, from the sound of it."

My face flushes again. Busted. "Oh, that? That was just Juliet being Juliet. You know how she loves to gossip."

Mark sits down on the edge of the bed, his expression turning serious.

"About the hotwife thing, you mean? With Ana and the others?"

I nod, not trusting my voice.

He's quiet for a moment, studying my face. "And what do you think about all that? The idea of being with another man while I watch?"

My breath catches in my throat. Is he really asking what I think he's asking? "I...I don't know," I stammer. "I guess I've never really considered it before our friends started trying it."

Mark reaches out and takes my hand, his thumb stroking over my knuckles. "But you are considering it now."

It's not a question.

I swallow hard, forcing myself to meet his gaze. "Maybe a little," I admit, my voice barely above a whisper. "Does that make me a terrible wife?"

To my surprise, Mark smiles. "No, baby. It makes you human. We all have fantasies, desires. It's natural to be curious."

I blink at him, stunned. "So...you're not mad? Or jealous?"

He shrugs. "I mean, the idea of you being desired, wanted by other men...it's kind of a turn-on, in a weird way."

"Really?" I breathe, hardly daring to believe it.

"Really." He leans in and kisses me softly, his lips warm and familiar. "I love you. I want you to be happy, fulfilled. If exploring this kink is something you want, then I'm willing to talk about it."

Tears prick at the corners of my eyes, and I surge forward to kiss him again, deeper this time. "I love you too. So much."

Mark grins against my lips. "If we do this, I have some ground rules."

I nod, willing to agree to anything. "Such as?"

He nips at my bottom lip, his hand sliding up my thigh. "Well, for starters...I get to pick the guy."

A surprised giggle escapes me. "Oh, is that so?"

"Mmm hmm." His fingers dance along the lace edge of my panties. "And I get to watch."

Arousal zings through my core, and I let my thighs fall open in invitation. "I can live with that."

"Good." Mark slips his hand inside my panties, finding me already slick and swollen. "Because you're mine. No matter who fucks this pussy, you'll always belong to me."

I moan as he strokes me, my hips rocking up to meet his touch. "Yes, baby. Always."

Mark kisses me hungrily, his tongue sweeping into my mouth, claiming me. As our passion escalates, I momentarily pull away, breathless. "Wait, where are the kids?"

"They're still asleep, baby. We've got time," Mark growls, pushing me back onto the bed with rough, possessive movements that make me gasp into his mouth as his fingers continue to work my clit. The thought of him watching someone fuck me turns me on. I wrap my legs around his waist, desperate to feel him inside me, but Mark chuckles and withdraws his hand.

He sits back on his heels, grinning down at me, and slowly licks my arousal off his fingers. "Jesus, you're fucking sexy when you're turned on," he says, his voice thick with desire.

I reach for him, aching to be filled again, but Mark bats my hand away with a smirk. "Not yet. Beg me to let you be a hotwife and I'll fuck you."

His words send a shiver of anticipation through me and I whisper with need. "Please, baby, please let me be a hotwife and please fuck me right now. I need you so bad."

His eyes simmers with barely contained desire. "Not yet."

He stands up and slides his shorts off, taking out his already-hard cock. "Make yourself come while you beg to be a hotwife, and then you'll get this." He strokes himself lazily, making sure I see.

Oh god, he's going to drive me insane with lust. My head is swimming as I spread my legs wider, slipping my own fingers inside my soaking wet pussy.

He's watching me, transfixed. "Do you wish your fingers were another man's cock?"

His question turns me on, and I slide a second finger into my pussy, imagining that he's watching someone fucking me. "God yes, I want someone to fuck me hard and make me your hotwife."

My own fingers aren't enough, and I stare at his cock while he strokes it. He's so damn hard. He needs to shove it in me. I'm going to explode if I don't get fucked. "Please, I need your cock."

Mark positions himself between my legs and continues to stroke himself while I start rubbing fast circles on my clit, desperate to come. He's watching my hands, and moans, "Fuck, you look so hot. Do you want to be a slut for someone else? Say it."

I start to unravel. "I want to be a hotwife. Please let me be a slut for you and another man. Let them fuck me however they want. Please!"

Mark slides into me in one hard thrust. He grabs my ankles and lifts them to his shoulders and slams into me over and over.

"Fuck, don't stop. Don't stop!" The world around me fades as the pleasure intensifies and I'm ready to combust. I grab my own breasts, tweaking my nipples hard, which sets me off. I cry out as my orgasm surges through me. "Mark, fuck!"

Mark slows and savors each slow stroke while he whispers, "That's my girl."

I writhe under him as pleasure zips from my fingers to my toes. When my spasms finally subside, Mark picks up speed again, chasing his own release. He feels so fucking good. I whimper, my nerve endings overloading, my mind barely able to comprehend the intensity of everything.

He grunts, "Oh god, I'm coming," as he explodes. He buries himself in me as deep as he can, his hips jerking as he unloads. The warmth of his cum sends a delicious shiver down my spine. Gasping and trembling, we melt into a heap of satisfied exhaustion.

Mark rolls over, pulling me close and pressing a kiss to my forehead. "Thank you."

I smile at him, dazed. "For what?"

He chuckles and nuzzles my neck, his stubble sending sparks dancing across my skin. "For indulging me, for playing along. And for trusting me."

My heart swells with love for him. "I'd do anything for you."

Mark gives me a lopsided grin, his eyes twinkling. "Yeah, and now you're going to be my hotwife."

"Am I?" I raise an eyebrow, trying to pretend I'm not ready to dance around the room in happiness.

"Hell yes, you are." Mark runs a hand down my side, coming to rest on the curve of my hip. "This isn't a game. I really want to share you. If you're up for it."

I study his face, looking for any trace of hesitation or doubt. But all I see is eagerness and desire. "I am."

Mark gives me a fierce kiss. "Just remember, I get to pick the guy."

I grin, anticipation fluttering in my stomach. "Yes, baby. It's your choice."

"Damn straight it is." He kisses me again, his touch soft and gentle this time.

I lie there in Mark's arms, basking in the afterglow and realizing this is the first time I've felt truly connected to him in a while. If this is what being a hotwife does for us, it's better than fucking another guy. I can't believe the turn my life has taken in just 24 hours. Yesterday, I was a bored housewife longing for more. Today, I'm a woman on the brink of becoming a hotwife with a husband who loves me enough to indulge my deepest fantasies. Does life get better than this?

The next few days pass in a blur of work deadlines, preschool pickups, and endless loads of laundry. But through it all, my mind keeps drifting back to my conversation with Mark. I'm surprised he's actually open to the idea of me sleeping with another man. More than open, even—he's genuinely turned on by the thought, and it's a side of him I've never seen before. I'm getting a glimpse of the kinky depths lurking beneath his calm, steady exterior.

Part of me is terrified at the prospect of actually going through with it. What if I chicken out at the last minute? What if the reality doesn't live up to the fantasy? What if it changes things between me and Mark in a way we can't come back from?

But another part of me—the part that's been lying dormant for far too long—is thrumming with excitement at the possibilities. The chance to be someone else for a night, someone wild and wanton and free. To be desired and pushed to the limits of my pleasure. It's a heady prospect, one that has me squirming in my office chair as I try to focus on budget reports.

Mark has been dropping little hints all week, sly comments about a surprise he has for me next weekend, but he's been maddeningly vague on the details. By the time Friday rolls around, I'm a bundle of nerves and anticipation. I don't know what he has planned, but I hope it involves sharing me.

As we're getting ready for bed, Mark comes up behind me at the bathroom sink and wraps his arms around my waist. He meets my eyes in the mirror, a mischievous glint in his gaze.

"So, I have some news," he murmurs, nuzzling into my neck. "My parents have agreed to babysit all night tomorrow."

My heartbeat quickens, and I lean back into his solid warmth. "Oh? And what's the occasion?"

Mark grins, his hands sliding up to cup my breasts through my thin cotton tank top. "Well, I was thinking...maybe it's time to test out this hotwife thing."

I suck in a sharp breath, my nipples tightening under his palms. "With who?"

He pinches my nipples lightly, making me gasp. "I invited Brandon over for dinner."

"Brandon?" I echo, my mind racing. Brandon is Mark's best friend and was the best man at our wedding. I'd be lying if I said I hadn't noticed his rugged good looks or the way his eyes sometimes linger on me. "Are you serious?"

Mark turns me around to face him, his expression soft but intense. "Oh yeah, baby. I trust Brandon, and more importantly, I trust you. If we're going to do this, I want it to be with someone we're both comfortable with."

I search his face for any hint of hesitation or doubt, but all I see is love and a glimmer of unmistakable heat. "And you're sure you're okay with this? With me and Brandon?"

He kisses me hard, his tongue delving deep into my mouth. I melt against him, my body responding instinctively to his touch. When he pulls back, we're both breathing heavily.

"More than okay. Brandon thinks you're gorgeous and says I'm the luckiest SOB in the world. I can't fucking wait to watch him make you come."

His words make me tremble, and my thighs press together against the ache building between them. "Jesus, Mark. Keep talking like that and I won't make it till tomorrow."

He chuckles, his hand slipping into my sleep shorts to cup my mound. "Oh, you'll make it because I have very specific plans for you. And they all involve you being a very, very good girl and saving this sweet pussy for our guest."

I whimper as he circles my clit with feather-light strokes, never quite giving me the pressure I need. "You're a fucking tease, you know that?"

"Yep, and think about this. I told him you've always wanted to be called filthy names, and he said that's his specialty." He nips at my earlobe, making me shiver. "Now get that sexy ass in bed. I want you well-rested for your big debut."

I let him lead me to the bed, my mind spinning with the thoughts of getting the dirty talk I've always craved. Every time Mark has tried to talk dirty, we've dissolved into a fit of giggles. He's just not dominant enough to pull it off. Holy hell, by this time tomorrow, I'll have had another cock inside me for the first time in over a decade. The thought is terrifying and exhilarating all at once.

As I drift off to sleep in Mark's arms, I can't help but wonder what Brandon will be like as a lover. If this is my only chance to fuck another guy, I hope he's rough and just takes what he wants.

Goddamn, I can't wait.

Chapter 3

As I get ready for the big dinner with Mark and Brandon, a flurry of emotions swirls inside me: excitement, nervousness, anticipation. I take extra care with my appearance, wanting to look my absolute best. After much deliberation, I choose a stunning yellow dress that hugs my curves in all the right places. The fitted bodice accentuates my full bust before flowing into a playful swing skirt that dances around my legs, ending just below the knees. The vibrant color glows against my brown skin. I style my hair in a braid-out and slip on my favorite strappy sandals. I can't remember the last time I took this much effort on my appearance, and the mirror tells me it was worth it. I look and feel sexy.

I descend the stairs and enter the kitchen to find Brandon already seated at the table. He rises to greet me, his eyes sparkling with appreciation. Brandon is a striking figure—tall, broad-shouldered, with close-cropped hair, strong brows, and a hint of stubble shadowing his chiseled jawline.

"June, you're absolutely radiant," Brandon says, the rumble of his words igniting a fire low in my belly.

Mark comes over and slips an arm around my waist, pulling me close. "She does. I'm the luckiest man alive." He places a soft kiss on my cheek, his breath warm against my skin. "Honey, why don't you fix some drinks for you and Brandon while I finish up in here?"

I flash Mark a smile. "Sure thing," I reply. Knowing that Brandon has given up alcohol, and wanting to keep my own head clear for the evening, I consider our options. My eyes light up as an idea strikes me.

"I could make us some fruity mocktails," I suggest, turning to face Brandon. "Any preference?"

Brandon gives me a playful grin. "I'm easy, so surprise me. I trust your judgment."

"Careful what you wish for," I joke as I lead him into the den.

As I mix our drinks, Brandon and I chat, catching up on life and work, but an undercurrent of tension simmers between us. The weight of his stare excites me as I move about the room. His gaze is like a physical caress. My fingers tremble slightly as I give him his drink, a telltale flush creeping up my neck.

Dinner is a lively affair, full of laughter and reminiscing as Mark and Brandon trade stories from their younger days. As I join in the merriment, butterflies swirl in my stomach from eagerness and uncertainty of what to expect tonight. I'm hyper-aware of Brandon's presence, the weight of his gaze, the accidental brush of his leg against mine under the table. Each casual touch sends sparks of electricity crackling through me until I'm practically vibrating with desire.

Once we finish dessert, Mark sits back in his chair and looks from me to Brandon and back again, a mischievous twinkle in his eye. "So, are we really doing this? Because if so, I want to see my gorgeous wife beg to be fucked."

Brandon leans forward, his expression intense. "I'm in if June is." He turns the full force of his attention on me. "What do you say? Ready to be a little slut for me and do as you're told?"

My brain blips out for a second at the men's words. Oooh, maybe Brandon really is good at dirty talk. Arousal floods my core, confirming I'm completely on board for tonight's adventure. I take a shaky breath and meet Brandon's smoldering gaze. "Yes, I'm ready."

Mark reaches over and squeezes my hand. "That's my girl," he says proudly. He stands up, pulling me to my feet and into his arms for a deep, passionate kiss that leaves me breathless. Then he releases me and grins at Brandon. "Let's move the party to the bedroom."

Brandon rises from his seat with barely restrained hunger. "Lead the way."

As we head upstairs, excitement thrums through my veins. Mark leads us down the hallway, but instead of turning into our usual bedroom, he guides us to the spare room at the end of the hall. Curiosity mingles with the butterflies in my stomach. Mark seems to have planned tonight out, which tells me he really does want this.

Mark pushes open the door and gestures for us to enter. As I step inside, my eyes widen. Soft, flickering candlelight gives the room a warm, intimate glow. The bed is stripped of the comforter, and there's fresh, crisp white sheets waiting to get messed up. But what really catches my attention is the tall director's chair positioned at the foot of the bed, offering a perfect view of the mattress.

I glance at Mark, a smile tugging at my lips. "Planning on directing us?"

His eyes twinkle. "What can I say? I want the best seat in the house for the show."

As Mark settles into the chair, I'm suddenly struck by the eroticism of having him watch my every move, every reaction. It adds a whole new layer of intensity to the situation. Fuck, this is hot.

Brandon moves to stand behind me. "You've been driving me crazy all night in that dress," he murmurs, his deep voice wrapping around me like a velvet embrace. "I've been dying to peel it off you, inch by delicious inch."

My breath hitches as his fingers graze my shoulder, tracing the delicate strap of my dress. With deliberate slowness, he eases it down, his touch igniting sparks beneath my skin. "Mark's a lucky man, getting to un-wrap you every night," he continues, his lips brushing along the sensitive nerves on my ear. "But tonight, you're all mine. And I intend to savor every" —he punctuates each word with a soft kiss along the column of my neck—"single"—another kiss, lower, his stubble rasping deliciously against my skin—"second."

I moan and tilt my head to the side, giving him better access. I didn't expect seduction, but this is wonderful. Brandon slides the other strap down, his movements unhurried, almost reverent. The bodice of my dress loosens and slips, revealing the lacy white bra beneath. For some reason, I expected Brandon to drag me up here and pound into me. The slow and sensual way he's undressing me leaves me wonderfully off balance, and I don't know how to react.

"Gorgeous," Brandon breathes as his hands skim down my arms, leaving goosebumps in their wake. "I love that you dressed up for me. But as pretty as this dress is, I'll like you even better out of it."

In one smooth motion, he unzips my dress and lets it pool at my feet. Cool air kisses my bare skin, and I shiver—not just from the cold, but also the heat of my husband's gaze.

Mark lets out a low whistle of appreciation. "You're a vision, baby. Brandon, don't you agree our June is sexy?"

"Oh, no doubt." Brandon's hands brush up my sides, his thumbs skimming the undersides of my breasts through the thin lace of my bra. I arch into his touch, craving more. "In fact, I'm going to enjoy using your toy."

Oh, fuck. The mix of worship and dirty talk is messing with my head and making me even more turned on. I lock eyes with Mark, and the raw hunger flickering in them as his friend works my nipples tells me I can let go and enjoy myself. My consciousness drifts towards a place of willing surrender...I want to be a toy for both of them.

Brandon turns me to face him, his eyes burning into mine. One hand comes up to cup my cheek, his thumb tracing the curve of my lower lip. "Tell me what you want, beautiful," he urges softly. "Don't be shy. This is all about your pleasure tonight, and I want to make sure you get what you need."

I wet my lips, my tongue darting out to taste the tip of his thumb.

Brandon's eyes flare, and he inhales sharply.

Can I really have whatever I want? There's only one way to find out. Emboldened, I hold his gaze. "I want you to use me and do whatever you want to me, call me dirty names, make me mindless so I'll forget anything outside of this bedroom."

When I hear my own words, I realize that being mindless is really what I need—beyond just the dirty talk. My brain is continually working overtime. I want to stop thinking and just experience pleasure. Since Mark and I have been so busy, it's been difficult to get the sense of freedom that only a really good fucking can bring me.

Brandon gives me a wicked grin of approval. "I like a woman who knows what she wants. And lucky for you, you're about to get it."

He unhooks my bra, letting it fall to the floor before he leans down and takes a nipple into his mouth briefly. Pleasure floods through me at the contact. I push my breasts closer to him, aching for more, but he stops sucking and commands, "I want you on the bed, on all fours. Face your man so he can see your reactions."

I immediately comply, the authority in his tone thrilling me to the core. As I settle on the bed, I meet my husband's gaze. He looks beyond turned on, and it makes everything that Brandon is doing so much better.

"Fucking hell, that ass is perfect," Brandon growls behind me. I hear the rustling of clothing as he undresses, followed by the thud of his belt buckle hitting the floor. I steal another glance at Mark and catch him stroking his erection through his jeans. My entire body shudders with longing. This is so dang filthy, and I'm desperate to feel a cock that isn't my husband's.

Brandon kneels on the bed behind me. He slips my panties off and spreads me open. "Jesus Christ, I have to get a closer look at this pussy," he murmurs, and before I can process what's happening, he buries his face in my slick folds with a deep groan.

I cry out at the sudden sensation of his tongue on my clit and the scratch of his beard against my pussy. My head spins from delight as I push back onto his hungry mouth. He moans into me, a noise of pure lust, as if he can't get enough of my taste. Pleasure ripples through me as he licks and sucks on my clit.

He comes up for air long enough to say, "The smell and taste of you are fucking addictive. Your husband is a lucky man to get to eat this pussy anytime he wants."

The filthiness of the comment sends another surge of liquid heat flooding from my core. I didn't know it was possible to be this turned on, to be desired and owned in a way that satisfies some deep, primal part of my brain. My eyes meet Mark's again, and his hooded gaze is filled with fire as he watches Brandon pleasure me.

The whole experience is incredibly hot, and I never break eye contact with Mark as his friend makes me writhe and moan in ecstasy. My breath is coming in shallow gasps and my toes curl as the pressure builds low in my belly, begging for release. Suddenly, one of Brandon's long, thick fingers pushes slowly inside me. I grip the sheets, overwhelmed by the intrusion.

"Fuck, you're so tight," Brandon groans. "This sweet cunt is just swallowing me up."

He starts finger-fucking me at a slow, steady rhythm, and I whimper. When his lips close around my clit, I come apart. "Ooooh, god!"

Mark stands and moves to sit beside me on the bed, cupping my face and kissing me fiercely as I shudder through the aftershocks of my orgasm. Our tongues tangle, and having my husband's lips on mine while his friend's face is buried in my pussy is so damn filthy.

When my spasms subside, Mark pulls back, his expression intense. "Baby, that was the sexiest thing I've ever seen. Seeing you lose control like that—I could watch that all day."

"We're just getting started," Brandon rasps from behind me, rising up and wrapping one arm around my waist to pull me flush with him.

As Mark sits down again, Brandon lines up his cock, the blunt head nudging my entrance, and my breath catches in my throat as I realize just how big he is. "Holy fuck."

He thrusts into me in one fluid movement, bottoming out in one go. I wail as he stretches me impossibly wide, the slight sting of pain adding another dimension to my pleasure. His cock is amazing, like nothing I've ever experienced before. He holds still for a moment, letting me adjust to the new sensation.

Mark laughs, delighted. "Oh, did I forget to mention that Brandon has a big cock?"

My head spins as I slowly rock my hips, gasping, "Yeah, you might have forgotten that bit."

Mark just laughs again as Brandon withdraws fully and then drives into me hard. I lower my head to the bed, crying out and clawing at the sheets as he sets a punishing pace. All I can do is hold on as he fucks me senseless, every stroke of his thick cock rubbing against my inner walls just right. I'm so overcome with pleasure my brain is melting.

"Such a good girl," Brandon says with a groan as he reaches forward and tangles one hand in my hair, tilting my head back and forcing me up onto my hands again. He growls, "Look at you, taking my cock like a champ. Does it feel good?"

"Uh-huh," I pant. The sensations coursing through me are indescribable. Every nerve ending zings with bliss. I'm completely consumed by Brandon, willing to be nothing more than a receptacle for his desire. The depth of my submission sends a wave of heat rushing through me as a second orgasm starts to build.

"I knew you'd like being a slut for my fat cock," Brandon grunts. "Now be a good girl and come for me."

Those dirty words send me over the edge. "Yes!" I wail as another climax hits, and my inner muscles clench down around Brandon's shaft.

"Such a good little cocksleeve," he grunts as he maintains his rhythm.

It takes all my focus to continue riding his cock through the waves of pleasure, and my arms shake as I struggle to keep from collapsing to the bed again. Mark's watching everything we do, and the anticipation building between us is a tangible force. His eyes darken with lust, mirroring my own desires. I can see the rapid rise and fall of his chest as he rubs himself through his jeans.

Brandon's rough hands grasp my hips, his fingers digging into my skin in a way that sends jolts of pleasure mixed with a hint of pain coursing through my body. His touch is commanding, and I don't want this to end.

"You ready to be a good little fucktoy and take all my cum?" His voice, brimming with primal hunger, leaves me weak-kneed and dizzy.

The word 'fucktoy' reverberates through my mind, sending a thrill of excitement through me. I want to be that for them tonight–a mindless, pleasure-filled toy. "Yes, please," I whimper, and Brandon's answering chuckle is dark, almost wicked, as he gives my hips a firm squeeze.

"That's a good girl," he purrs, igniting a delicious warmth throughout my body

Mark's gaze never leaves mine, his expression a mix of desire, love, and a hint of possessiveness. "You're so beautiful like this, baby," he murmurs, his voice thick with desire. "Our very own pretty little slut." His words make my heart race, a flood of warmth spreading through me at his praise, and I moan at how depraved I am.

Brandon joins in. "She's such a pretty little cumslut for us to enjoy." His words burn like a delicious fire, the degradation swirling with the impact of his praise.

The combination of Brandon's rough fucking and the dirty talk from both men sends me spiraling. I can feel another orgasm building, and it's all I can do to keep breathing. I lock eyes with Mark, my gaze pleading for his permission to crash over that sweet edge. He sees it, and a wicked smile quirks his lips upwards. "Come again for us, babygirl," he orders, and my climax slams through me, making me scream in ecstasy.

My cry of pleasure makes Brandon change his angle, hitting a new sweet spot deep inside me and intensifying the bliss. Waves of rapture assault me, and I tighten around him, my body trembling in anticipation of another orgasm.

When Brandon speaks, it takes me a second to realize he's talking to Mark. "You like watching me fuck your wife, don't you? Look at how much she loves my cock."

I'm momentarily shocked, and my eyes fly to Mark to see how he's taking it. Mark's response is a low groan, his eyes never leaving the sight of Brandon fucking me. I can see the desire in his gaze, the hunger, and I know that he's enjoying this just as much as I am. It fuels my own desire, and I thrust back against Brandon, eager for more.

The sound of our bodies slapping together fills the room, punctuated by my moans and Brandon's grunts. I'm continually on the edge, knowing I could explode again at any second. I'm not sure how much more I can take, but at the same time, I never want this to end. Brandon continues to fuck me, hitting that sweet spot over and over again. I close my eyes, lost in the bliss—finally achieving what I wanted. I'm mindless and just a hole for them to fuck.

Right when I'm about to come again, Brandon pulls out and flips me onto my back. With one swift motion, he plunges back into me, bottoming out as I moan. I wrap my legs around him and hold onto his arms. His pace is relentless, driving into me over and over again. My tits bounce in time with his forceful thrusts, leaving me as powerless as a rag doll in his grasp.

His powerful strokes flood me with pleasure, my orgasm building steadily but remaining just out of reach. "Please, Brandon," I beg, my voice trembling. "Please, let me come again."

Brandon slows down, and it's suddenly worse; every stroke is a wonderful agony as he massages every inch of my insides.

"Does our fucktoy want to come?" Brandon's tone is teasing.

I thrash against him. "Please, oh god, please let me come. I need it."

"Then come for us. Do it now before I come, or it will be too late."

What? No? Brandon's thrusts become more erratic, his grip on my hips tightening to the point of bruising. I can feel his cock swelling inside me, the tremors of his impending orgasm evident in his ragged breaths.

Just knowing he's so close tips me over the edge again, and I come undone. I scream out as my orgasm tears through me like a tidal wave. White spots dance along the corners of my vision, and I convulse around him. The pleasure is so intense it borders on pain. My pussy clenches, milking his cock as the waves of pleasure consume me.

As I ride out my orgasm, I can hear Mark's voice, filled with desire and love. "That's my good girl. Our pretty little slut." His words send a thrill through me.

Brandon groans, and with a few sharp whacks against my sensitive pussy, he erupts. His entire body shudders as the ropes of his warm sticky cum fill me. As he continues to unload, his face a mask of pure enjoyment, a sense of accomplishment washes over me for having satisfied him so thoroughly.

When he's finished, he leans down to kiss me, his lips brushing against mine softly. "Good girl," he whispers, and I bask in his praise.

I glance over at Mark, seeing the desire in his gaze, the hunger that mirrors my own. I know that he's next, that he's eager to claim me for himself. I'm not going to feel complete until he's inside me, but I want to enjoy the euphoria a few minutes longer.

My body is humming with pleasure as I listen to Mark and Brandon talk. I'm in a happy, floaty place, and my mind is blissfully empty. I close my eyes and let myself drift.

CHAPTER 4

The sound of rustling clothing brings me back to reality as I lie sprawled on the bed, still fuzzy from my numerous orgasms. My skin is flushed and sensitive, the cool air from the vent sending goosebumps up and down my body. I sink into the softness of the sheets, my eyes fluttering open to gaze upon Brandon and Mark. Brandon is getting dressed while Mark sits beside me, a feral fire igniting in his eyes. He wants me — desperately. He's just waiting for Brandon to leave.

Brandon leans down and kisses me softly. "Thank you for a wonderful time," he murmurs, his voice low and sexy. "You were amazing."

"You were too," I whisper, and we smile at each other as he gathers his things and heads for the door.

Right before he leaves, he pauses and smirks at Mark. "Take care of our pretty little slut. She deserves to be well taken care of for being such a good girl." He winks at us as he exits the room, leaving us alone.

As soon as we hear the front door shut, Mark's hands are all over me, his mouth crashing against mine as his fingers explore my body. My hands tangle in his hair, tugging at the strands as he groans in pleasure. We undress him in a flurry, our entwined bodies rolling and tangling in the sheets. We're both wild for each other, consumed with passion. I need him NOW.

He pushes my legs apart, nudging his cock against my entrance before teasing my clit with the tip. I gasp, arching my back as he presses inside me, every inch of his cock filling me up. His hand grips my hip as he thrusts hard and deep, each movement sending waves of pleasure from my fingertips to my toes.

"You're mine," he growls, his voice rough and possessive. "MY good girl. Mine to fuck and pleasure. Mine to fill with cum."

"Yes, yours," I moan, my mind reeling with delight. His fingers find my clit, circling the sensitive nub as he continues to thrust. I can feel my body building towards another release, the tension coiling tight inside me.

Our sweat-slicked bodies slide against each other as he pounds into me, our movements growing more frantic. I wrap my legs around him, my fingers digging into his back as he brings me to the edge of my release.

"Come for me," he commands, his voice thick with desire. "Come for your husband. Show me how much you love it when I fuck you."

His words send me crashing over the edge, my body convulsing around his cock as I cry out his name. He follows closely behind, his release filling me up as he groans against my neck. We lie there, tangled in each other's arms, the sound of our panting filling the silence.

As our bodies cool and our breathing returns to normal, Mark gazes into my eyes, his expression filled with love and adoration. "You were amazing tonight. I'm so proud of you for being such a good girl for us."

His words fill me with joy, and I smile at him. "I loved every moment of it," I admit, kissing him softly. "Brandon was the perfect choice. You know me so well. And I'd do this again, just say the word."

There's a wicked gleam in his eyes. "I'm going to want this again, but not until I've had a couple weeks of fucking you and reminding you I'm the only one you love, no matter how many other guys you fuck."

A happy warmth fills me, and I giggle. "You are the only one I love. Forever."

He growls again, possessively, and my head spins as he kisses me deeply. I never expected fucking someone else would bring this side out in Mark, but I can tell our marriage is revitalized. Being a hotwife is fucking amazing.

The End

July Hotwife

Hotwife of the Month Book 7

Lacey Cross

CHAPTER 1

I'm sprawled out on a lounge chair facing the ocean at a luxurious Bali resort. As I inhale the salty tang of the ocean air mixed with the coconut scent of my suntan lotion, I finally relax for the first time in weeks. God, I needed this vacation. It's been a stressful year.

I feel dumb to even have complaints, and sometimes it feels like I have no one to talk to. I'm not sure my friends would understand since I have a fabulous life. I'm thirty-five, and I have a wonderful husband who dotes on me and more money than I need to live comfortably. But I've had a gnawing pit in my stomach ever since I sold my social media company a few months ago. I should be over the moon about it. Selling the company gave me the freedom to do whatever I want with my life. Instead, I feel...aimless.

The easiest answer is to just enjoy Bali and stop being a baby while on an incredible vacation with the man I love. My husband, Arthur, loves to surf, and he's been doing it since he was young. We take a couple of trips every year to different locations so he can play in the ocean while I enjoy the amenities of the resort spa and try to relax.

I sigh and watch the small figures paddling in the ocean. From this distance, I can't tell which one is Arthur, but it doesn't matter. As I watch a surfer catch a wave and ride it expertly to the shore, I feel a twinge of envy. I love that Arthur has a passion and a hobby, but I'm just...lounging. My career was everything, and now I have no purpose, no direction, and it's driving me fucking crazy. I'm usually vivacious and confident about my place in life, but now I'm second guessing everything—everything except my marriage, even though we've been going through a rough patch in the last year.

I turn my attention to the other beachgoers, my mind hungry for distraction. The resort is adjacent to a public beach, and a group of college-aged kids are playing volleyball close by. Their laughter and good-natured trash talk carries over the sound of the waves. I smile at their antics, remembering my own wild days of partying in college. God, when was the last time I let loose like that? I have a wonderful group of friends, but our monthly meetup while our husbands play cards in the basement doesn't exactly count as letting loose.

A young couple strolls by, hand in hand, their eyes locked on each other like they're the only two people in the world. I feel a pang in my chest, a longing for that kind of connection and passion. Arthur and I used to be like that, once upon a time. But now, it feels like we're just going through the motions, living our comfortable, luxurious life.

Yeah, I need to get out of this funk. I need a change, an adventure, something to make me feel alive again...or maybe I just need a good hard pounding from my husband. He's been busy with work too, and other than his desire to surf, we plan on using this trip to reconnect.

Fuck it, no more moping around. Standing up, I adjust my flowing sundress and slip my sandals on. I'm determined to be happy and have fun. I'm going to start by seducing my husband, and then I'm going to do something on this trip that's daring, something that scares me. It's time to live a little.

Arthur is still out on the water, so I climb the rocky steps towards the resort's outside bar. I need to get out of my head and a fruity drink should help. As I approach, I catch my reflection in a mirrored pillar. My naturally tan skin is glowing, my hair tousled by the sea breeze, and my blue sundress is sexy. For a moment, I hardly recognize myself because I actually look relaxed. There's a spark in my eyes that I haven't seen in years, a hint of the wild, carefree woman I used to be before I became Juliet, the business woman and life of every party. Hey, I guess vacation is actually working its magic on me.

I perch on a barstool, and a bartender offers me the daily special drink–it's delicious. I'm enjoying the tropical flavors and having fun people watching...and that's when I spot him: a guy, maybe a few years younger than me, with scruffy blonde hair and a body that screams surfer. He catches my eye and raises his drink in a friendly toast.

Before I know it, he's sauntering over. "Mind if I join you?" he asks, his voice a low rumble that sends a shiver down my spine.

I bet this guy hangs around at bars to pick up wealthy women. He has the demeanor of someone who's just looking for a good time. I can feel my body responding to him. Yeah, he's attractive enough he probably gets plenty of women. I try to play it cool. "Go ahead."

He slides onto the stool next to me, his bare arm brushing against mine and giving me goosebumps. "I'm Kai," he says, flashing a smile that could melt the panties off a grandma. "And you are?"

"Juliet." I'm surprised by how breathy my voice sounds.

"Juliet," he repeats, like he's savoring the taste of my name. "So, what brings a goddess like you to this humble island?"

I can't help but laugh. "Goddess? That's a bit much, don't you think?"

He grins, leaning in closer. "Just calling it like I see it. But you didn't answer my question."

Kai has a fresh linen smell that I enjoy. I swirl my drink and play coy. "Oh, you know, the usual. Escaping reality, seeking adventure. All that good stuff."

I know I'm being flirty, but Arthur and I have a pact. He enjoys it when I flirt with other guys and get worked up for him. He says as long as I eat at home, he doesn't care where I get my appetite. With how sexy Kai is, I'm going to have a nice appetite when I seduce my husband later.

Kai's eyes sparkle with mischief. "Adventure, huh? Well, you've come to the right place. And maybe found the right person."

Damn, this guy is smooth, though I'm sure he knows it. I raise an eyebrow. "Is that so? And what kind of adventures are you offering?"

He leans in even closer. "How about we start with a midnight swim under the stars?"

My heart races at the suggestion, and I suddenly wonder if he has a big cock—not that I'm going to find out. I manage to keep my voice steady. "Tempting, but I'm not sure my husband would approve."

Kai's eyes drop to my wedding ring, but his smile doesn't falter. "Ah, the plot thickens. Well, how about a raincheck then? If you and your husband ever want an adventure..."

He leaves his sentence hanging, and my breath catches while pleasure swirls in my core. Is he talking about a threesome? I refuse to ask for clarification since that would make it seem like I'm interested.

Kai doesn't press for anything more, and we continue chatting. I find myself laughing more than I have in months. Kai's quick wit matches my own, and our banter flows effortlessly. As we talk, I'm acutely aware of the wedding ring on my finger. I love Arthur, I really do. But there's something about Kai that is making me feel more alive than I have in a long time...which means I need to get out of here and find my husband.

Just as I'm debating how to make an excuse and leave, I hear Arthur's voice behind me. "There you are, Juliet," he says, his hand landing on my shoulder.

I turn to face him, my heart pounding. His hair and clothes are still damp from the ocean, and he has a towel draped over his arms. He smells briny, so different from the clean and fresh scent of Kai. Arthur's eyes flick from me to the surfer, a question in his gaze.

Kai takes that moment to excuse himself by saying, "It was great meeting you, Juliet." He gives me one last meaningful look before disappearing into the crowd.

As I watch him go, I can't help but wonder what would have happened if I was single. I'd never cheat on Arthur–never in a million years–but Kai is the type of guy I'd fuck in a heartbeat if I wasn't married. Yeah, I need to stop thinking about that.

I give Arthur my sweetest smile as I stand up and link my arm with his. As we head back to our room, desire simmers in my core and the world seems full of possibilities. Why did flirting with one random guy at the bar suddenly make this vacation anything but ordinary?

I side eye my husband as we get off the elevator to our floor. Arthur is looking mighty sexy right now. It's time to enact Operation Seduce My Husband.

CHAPTER 2

Our room is just as opulent as the rest of the resort, with a massive four-poster bed draped in white linens, a private balcony overlooking the ocean, and a bathroom that looks like it belongs in a spa. The walls are adorned with local artwork, and a gentle sea breeze wafts through the open windows, carrying the salt-tinged air.

As soon as the door closes behind us, Arthur slips into the bathroom to shower while I kick my sandals off and wander out to the balcony and wait for him to get out so I can get his cock into me.

He's wearing a robe when he joins me on the balcony after his shower, and wraps his arms around me from behind. "I think my wife needs to remember who owns her," he murmurs, his breath warm against my neck.

Leaning back into him, I savor the feeling of his strong body against mine. I love it when he says stuff like this. He and I both know he doesn't really own me, but it's great when he gets possessive and growly. If flirting with Kai brought this out, maybe I need to flirt a lot on this trip.

I turn my head to give him a playful wink. "Babe, you know I only have eyes for you."

His hands slide down to my hips, pulling me closer and I can feel his erection against my ass. His voice is husky. "You know, we should probably test out that bed. Make sure it's up to our standards."

I laugh, spinning in his arms to face him. "Is that so? And how does that test work?"

His eyes darken with desire, and he leans in close, his lips barely brushing against mine. "I'll show you..." he whispers before capturing my mouth in a searing kiss.

He pulls me into the room and as we tumble onto the bed, I giggle. This is great. I didn't even have to seduce him. I pull at the tie on his robe, enjoying the softness of his freshly cleaned skin. His body is so familiar, almost like an extension of my own, and yet still desirable after all these years. Arthur tugs the straps of my sundress down my arms, exposing my breasts. He sucks on a nipple in the exact way I love, and I run my fingers through his hair and arch my back from the pleasurable pull in my core.

He lavishes attention on one breast before moving to the other. Ripples of delight head straight to my pussy the longer he worships my breasts, and I'm so wet I wish he'd get his cock in me. He slides the hem of my dress up and slips a hand between my legs, pushing aside my panties so he can brush circles around my clit. I cry out in ecstasy and almost come undone. Holy fuck, I'm already close to an orgasm. I swear vacation sex always feels better, and I don't know why.

I'm so lost in the joy of the moment that I almost don't understand what he's saying when he speaks. "Did you think about fucking that guy at the bar?"

I can hear the erotic tinge in his voice, and the lustful tone sends my arousal level through the roof. Holy shit, why is he asking about this when his finger is on my clit? He's watched me flirt with plenty of guys in the past, and he's always just smiled and given me that knowing look, secure in the knowledge that he's the only guy I want.

He continues circling my clit, and I moan, "Mmm, Kai? No. I wouldn 't..."

He gives a light pinch to my clit, and I cry out in pleasure and almost climax again. His voice is husky. "Don't start lying to me now. You were thinking about fucking him, weren't you?"

Lust burns through my brain, and I rock my hips against his hand. This might be the most delicious dirty talk he's ever engaged in, and I can have fun with this. I purr at him, "If I was, are you going to spank me?"

He laughs. "You'd like that too much. Maybe I just won't let you come until you admit you were thinking of fucking another man."

The pressure of his fingers on my clit intensifies, and I gasp in delight. My whole body is burning with need, and I'm so close to my orgasm I can taste it. "Oh god, yes, I was. Please let me come, oh fuck."

My toes curl from pleasure as he nibbles on my ear lobe. "Tell me everything you thought about him. Don't make me stop."

"Fuck, he's hot but I only want you," I groan as I try to hold back my orgasm.

He pushes his fingers inside me as he continues rubbing my clit with his thumb. "Juliet..." The warning in his tone of voice sends a shiver down my spine. "You're lying."

He moves his fingers slower, making it so I can't come, and I gasp out, "No, no, I'm not."

He kisses up my neck until his lips are on my mouth, devouring my moans of pleasure. When he breaks off the kiss, his voice is rough. "Lie to me again and you won't get to come."

Oh god, I'll do anything to come. I whine in desperation, "I wondered what his cock looked like."

I feel him smirk against my skin as he rubs my clit in faster circles. "Anything else?"

I'm so far gone I start babbling. "He offered to take me on a midnight swim under the stars and said if you and I both wanted an adventure, to let him know."

He pulls back and studies me for a moment before finger fucking me harder. "Keep going," he rumbles, his voice dripping with lust.

"I didn't just wonder what his cock looked like, I wondered if it was big.

Oh, fuck, please don't stop!" My thigh muscles start quivering, and I'm barely able to hold back my orgasm. "Oh god, I'm going to come!"

"Not yet," he growls and removes his fingers right as I start to come.

I cry out from the stolen orgasm. Fuck, why did he stop?

He gives me a deep kiss with a "hold on, baby" and quickly discards his robe. He positions himself between my legs, and when he slides into my aching pussy, I cry out again, this time in relief.

"Whose cock do you want more?" he asks as he hammers into me.

I grip at his shoulders and wrap my legs around him. "Yours!" I'm panting and moaning loudly, already close to coming again.

He pounds me fast and hard. "Yeah? Mine?"

"Yes!"

"Only mine?"

"Oh, fuck, yes! Only yours! Always yours!" I cry out as my orgasm hits.

I dig my fingers into his shoulders, and my pussy tightens around his cock as the pleasure sweeps over me in waves. He doesn't slow down as I shudder beneath him. My climax seems to go on forever, and I can't get enough. When he finally comes, he groans and his cock pulses as he blows his load.

When he's done, he tumbles onto the bed next to me, pulling me into his arms. I nuzzle into him, pressing kisses to his collarbone and throat while he catches his breath. Mmm, this is a great start to our vacation.

His voice is rough when he speaks. "You're really hot when you're thinking about getting fucked by other men."

I swat playfully at his chest. "Hey, I wasn't the one who brought it up! You started it."

He grins at me, his eyes shining. "I like it when you flirt and another guy wants you since I know you're coming home with me."

I prop up on an elbow and draw a fingertip along the ridges of his abs, enjoying the way his body shivers in response to my touch. "Well, good, because I don't really want to fuck Kai."

He captures my hand and brings it up to his mouth, kissing each fingertip, before saying, "If you wanted to, we could talk about it."

I raise my eyebrow at him. "What if Kai's idea of an adventure is a threesome?"

That makes him laugh. "Yeah, I don't know about that, but I'd watch him fuck you."

This time it's me who giggles as I snuggle against him and hide my face in the crook of his arm. "Let me think about that."

"Okay, love." He strokes my back as we both fall silent, enjoying the post orgasmic haze. I'm too content right now to think about fucking another guy. This will have to wait until tomorrow.

Chapter 3

As soon as I wake up in the morning, all I can think about is Arthur's offer to let me fuck Kai. A lot of our friends are experimenting with the hotwife lifestyle, and I've daydreamed about doing it. I've known for weeks that if given the chance, I'd try it, but the thought scares me as well. If he brings it up again, I'll tell him I want to.

After a shower and breakfast, we go for a walk along the beach. We hold hands and he keeps smiling at me. I can tell he's thinking something, but he doesn't voice it. The third time I catch him grinning, I squeeze his hand and ask, "What?"

He's quiet for a long moment before answering. "You're incredible. And I want to give you whatever you need. You know that, right?"

I furrow my brows, confused. "Uh, yeah?"

"So, I really meant what I said last night. If you want to fuck that guy Kai from the bar, I'd like to watch."

His words send a rush of heat through my body, and my heart rate quickens. Oh god, I really do want to do it, even knowing it's scary, and Arthur wanting to watch makes the idea even more appealing. I'm about to tell him I'm interested when I spot Kai on the beach ahead of us, walking our way. My mind goes blank.

Arthur notices the way I freeze and glances in the same direction. His voice is tender as he whispers, "I love you. Nothing changes that, but this is your decision. Don't do anything you don't really want to do, okay?"

"I love you, too, babe." I pull him to me and kiss him passionately, letting all of the emotions I've felt these past few months–hell, the past few years–pour into it. The depth of this kiss is surprising, even to me, but I know that no matter what happens next, he's my anchor. I trust him so deeply, and that helps me relax. "I want to do it if he's okay with you watching."

Arthur hugs me tightly, kissing me once more before we separate, and we keep strolling hand in hand as we near Kai.

Kai smiles at us as we approach. "Hey, Juliet," he says casually, "I wasn't sure if we'd run into each other again."

I smile back at him, matching his casual tone. "I was going to look for you. My husband and I are interested in your offer of adventure."

Arthur pipes up, "Hey, I'm Arthur. Juliet mentioned your offer, but we'd need to discuss me watching her have some fun."

My eyes widen slightly. This is all happening so fast. When I look at Arthur, I see only love and trust in his eyes. And a bit of excitement. So, I turn back to Kai, whose grin grows even wider as he says, "Sure. This won't be the first time a husband has watched me with their wife."

Oh god, he's done this before. Why does that make it even hotter? The guys talk logistics while I daydream about what it's going to be like fucking another guy again after so many years. If I had known I'd become a hotwife on this trip, I would have been bouncing with excitement for days. When I hear them mention tonight, my heart rate speeds up as a wet heat builds between my legs. Holy fuck, tonight?

We agree to meet later on the beach, and the guys pull out their phones and exchange numbers. I'm practically buzzing with anticipation. As we walk away, Arthur is all smiles and holds me close. I can tell he's just as excited about this as I am.

I feel a strange mixture of horniness and uncertainty throughout the day, like I'm at a rollercoaster before I step into the seat. My imagination runs wild as I picture what's going to happen. Will Kai be able to make me come? What if Arthur doesn't like it? What if this ruins our marriage? I push those thoughts to the back of my mind. I trust Arthur, and I know he'll be honest with me if something is wrong. I just need to enjoy tonight.

I dress in a flowy, black dress with spaghetti straps that leave my shoulders bare. My hair is in one loose braid so the sea breeze doesn't mess it up too much. I'm applying a light touch of makeup when my cell phone pings with a message. I pick it up and see it's from my best friend, Ariel.

Ariel

> Hey, if you get bored in Bali, check out Debra's latest blog post. It's hilarious.

Debra is the wife of one of my husband's friends, and she's been getting on everyone's nerves with her slut shaming. With all our friends trying out the hotwife lifestyle, Debra seems to think we're all harlots. I don't know if she's religious, but it definitely seems like she's praying for our jezebel souls. Her latest thing is blogging anonymously to talk about the downfall of marriage due to the hotwife craze, but I know it's her. She got tipsy one night and showed me an article she wrote, so I followed her blog. I don't think she remembers showing it to me.

I'm curious about this post from Debra, but it'll have to wait. I giggle and type a quick reply to Ariel.

Juliet

> Oh, I will, but not tonight. I'm about to go fuck a hot surfer while Arthur watches.

Ariel's reply doesn't disappoint.

Ariel

> OMG, you too? Okay, you have to tell me everything when you get home, and I mean EVERYTHING.

I smile and promise a long gab session when I return. As soon as I set my phone down, Arthur comes into the bathroom behind me and puts his hands on my waist, gazing at our reflections in the mirror.

He murmurs, "I love you," and I lean back into him, resting my head on his shoulder. "I love you, too."

He presses a kiss to my cheek. "Now, let's get out there and have some fun."

I giggle as we leave the bathroom, and I slip on my sandals. It's time to do something daring that scares me.

CHAPTER 4

The beach at night is totally different than during the day since most of the tourists are busy elsewhere. There are a few groups of people, but everyone keeps to themselves and are wrapped up in enjoying their own company. Arthur leads me down the beach, and I realize he has a destination in mind. Hell, I guess I should have paid attention earlier when he and Kai were talking, but I was too busy daydreaming about cock.

Butterflies swirl in my stomach when I see Kai walking in our direction. He's in board shorts, an open white button-down shirt, and sandals. He's such a surfer cliche, and he looks just as amazing as earlier.

He flashes us a smile and falls in stride with us. "So, you all ready for an adventure?"

I'm suddenly shy, and I nod, not sure I trust my voice. Arthur claps him on the back and gives a little chuckle. "That we are, and thanks for the invitation."

We head down the beach together and my anticipation grows with each step. I could ask where they're taking me, but I'm enjoying the mystery. A small thrill travels through me as I realize that very soon, my husband is going to watch another man fuck me.

We round a sand dune and some large rocks, and Kai veers off towards stairs that lead to a stunning private villa with a pool overlooking the ocean.

Everything about this place screams wealth and luxury.

"Kai, where are we?" I say with wonder.

He shoots me a dazzling smile and takes my hand as we climb the stairs to the house. "I'm staying here for a few weeks. The view is incredible."

As he takes us through the house, I admire the luxurious decor and view from the floor-to-ceiling windows, and I suddenly realize I misjudged Kai. He's clearly got money. He's not just some guy who hangs out at bars to pick up wealthy tourists.

We head out to the pool where there is a firepit and several lounges. Even though it overlooks the ocean, it's secluded and no one can see us. The moonlight and the flickering lights from the lit torches lend a romantic feel to the space. He prepared for tonight.

Kai releases my hand and waves us over to the loungers. "Have a seat and I'll get us drinks."

I'd love a cocktail, but I want a clear head so I ask him to bring me water. Arthur and I take a seat next to each other, and I grin at him. "This is certainly different than I imagined."

"Good different, I hope."

I'm already so turned on I can't imagine it won't be great. I giggle and give him a playful shove. "Good different. I thought we were going to go to the beach, but this is nice. Like really nice."

He takes my hand and gives it a squeeze. "Just enjoy tonight. Promise?"

"I promise."

My heart swells with love for Arthur as Kai returns with glasses of water. He sets the water down on a table next to me before perching on the end of my lounger. I admire how gorgeous he is while we sip our water and make idle chatter about Bali and how amazing it is here. It's surprisingly not awkward as we all chat, and I learn more about Kai and how he loves surfing and exploring the world.

As the conversation winds down, Kai leans towards me with a flirty smile. "So, I offered you a midnight swim. Are you up for it?"

I nod and flush as Kai stands and offers me his hand. I'm usually the life of the party, but something about Kai makes me feel shy. But then again, I've never been in a situation like this, so should I really be surprised?

I let him pull me to my feet, and Arthur says, "I'm going to be right here, baby. Remember, this is for you to enjoy."

Smiling at Arthur, I blow him a kiss. I didn't really think Arthur would ever share me, and my heart beats wildly as I realize I'm about to fuck someone else for the first time since college, and I'm ready for it.

I turn my attention to Kai and gaze up at him. He steps closer to me and dips his head, bringing his mouth to mine. His kiss is gentle and searching, and I open to him without hesitation, curling my hands into the fabric of his open shirt.

As we kiss, my head spins. Knowing that Arthur is watching makes this oddly romantic and dirty at the same time. The kiss escalates into a deeper, more passionate exploration, and my whole body sings with desire. Kai tastes like cinnamon, and I'm suddenly desperate for him.

His hands slide to my ass, and he pulls me in tight as he devours my mouth. He's a skilled kisser, and as his tongue twirls with mine, I let myself go and enjoy the moment. When he breaks off the kiss and tugs me toward the water, I follow eagerly. Heck yeah, time to get naked and get some cock in me.

We stop at the edge of the pool, and Kai kisses me softly once again, murmuring, "You're so beautiful," and brushing a strand of hair back from my face. "Are you sure you want this?"

I nod, trying to keep my voice steady. "I've never been more sure of anything. Just fuck me already."

He laughs. "Impatient. I like that."

Kai slowly slips the straps of my dress down my shoulders, teasingly baring my breasts. The air is warm, but I still shiver as my nipples harden. I glance over at Arthur and see he's turned sideways in his chair, facing us with an intent expression as he watches.

Kai slides my dress down farther, and it pools around my feet. All I have on are my sandals and black lace panties. Goosebumps cover my skin as he peels my panties to my feet. I step out of them and kick my sandals off, leaving me completely bare. I expected a hurried fucking on a sand dune; instead, I feel like I'm being seduced while he's driving me crazy.

He grips my hips, and his voice is hoarse. "Before we start, I need to know what you want."

Oh god, I want him to just fuck me and not make me ask for it. I hesitate and when he makes no further moves, I know I have to say it. My mouth goes dry and I lick my lips, whispering, "I want your cock."

Kai smirks and lifts his voice. "I think your husband needs to hear what a little slut his wife is. Say it louder."

Heat rushes through me, and I almost moan. Making me say it aloud is so dang dirty. When I repeat myself, I speak up so Arthur can hear me. "I want your cock."

Kai cups my face and tips my chin up. "Next question. Do you want to be fucked hard or soft?"

Oooh, what? I didn't even consider anything beyond getting his cock inside me. My brain blips out for a moment. Do I dare ask for what I really want? Then it hits me. If I don't ask for it now, when will I? Now's my chance to experience something different.

Tilting my head slightly so I can see Arthur, I respond to Kai. "I want it hard." I take a deep breath and decide to add a plea to my answer. "Please...and I like dirty talk and being called names."

Arthur has a glazed look of lust on his face, but he smiles and nods at me. That's all I need.

Kai pinches my nipple, and a bolt of lust zings through me as I gasp and give him my attention again. He smirks. "Okay, then here's the rules, my little fucktoy."

I can feel my body flush at the word fucktoy. No one has ever called me that before.

His voice is firm and authoritative when he continues. "If you need me to stop for any reason, say red light. Got it?"

I'm already nodding before he's done talking. "Yes, got it. Red light."

The negotiation is making me even more desperate for his cock. Now that I know he's going to fuck me hard, I can feel my inner thighs getting damp.

"Then let's begin."

I'm about to ask what he wants me to do, but before I can say anything, he spins me around until I'm facing a patio chair and he pushes my shoulders down, bending me over. I grab the arms of the chair, confused. Aren't we going swimming?

When his hand lands on my ass in a sharp slap, I yelp in surprise. His voice is gruff. "Keep still. Your husband told me you enjoyed being spanked. He said it turned you into an obedient little slut."

Holy fuck. This is even better than I imagined. I'm guessing the guys were texting today, and I'm sure that Arthur didn't actually say it turned me into an obedient little slut, but I enjoy imagining he did. Kai slaps me a few more times, and my eyes close as I enjoy the sensations rippling through my body. I love Arthur's spankings, but Kai's are more intense.

As Kai spanks me harder, I gasp and wiggle my hips from the stinging pain, enjoying every second of it. I'm going to be a wet mess by the time he finally fucks me, and getting spanked by someone other than my husband makes me really feel like a slut.

I open my eyes to glance at Arthur, and my heart flutters. He's cupping himself through his pants, and his cock is bulging. I drop my head while I try to process the pleasure washing over me while Kai continues spanking me. My pussy is slick and needy, and I can feel myself getting fuzzy-headed. Maybe Arthur really did say it turned me into an obedient little slut because the longer Kai spanks me, the more compliant I get. He could ask me to do anything, and I'd probably do it.

I drift in a haze of pleasure, and when he stops spanking me, I hear rustling behind me. I see his clothes hit the pavement. He grabs my hip and uses his knees to force my legs apart. When the blunt head of his cock presses against my pussy, I suck in my breath. Holy fuck, I guess we aren't going swimming.

Kai plunges his cock into me, and I cry out, gripping the arms of the chair more tightly so I don't fall forward. Oh My God. He's huge. His cock stretches me out, and my head spins from delight as his thickness pings nerve endings I didn't even know I had.

He doesn't give me time to adjust as he starts thrusting hard with each stroke. His balls bounce against my clit, adding a hint of delicious extra sensation. He keeps hold of one hip, and I feel like a doll being tossed around as he fucks me furiously. My tits are bouncing, and my moans get louder as the rapture builds in layers.

Damn, this went from zero to 60 so fast, but I'm getting exactly what I wanted. With his free hand, he twists my braid in his fist, yanking my head back. I hiss from the erotic combination of pleasure and pain. "Oh god, please..." I moan, but I have no idea what I'm pleading for.

"What do you want, my fucktoy?" he taunts, increasing his tempo. The sound of his skin slapping against mine is obscene.

"Harder, I need it harder!"

He still has my hair gripped tightly in his fist, and when he tugs, it sends electric tingles across my scalp. I'm already close to coming, and I try to focus on holding off my orgasm. I whimper as my legs shake, and to distract myself from how good his cock feels, I tilt my head as much as I can so I can look at Arthur. He's resting back on the lounge and rubbing his cock through his jeans while he watches Kai pound my cunt. There's a look of pure bliss on his face. Oh god, I love this.

Seeing Arthur enjoying himself pushes me over the edge. I detonate around Kai's cock and cry out, "Oh fuck, oh fuck!"

Pleasure radiates from my core, and when Kai pulls his cock from my pussy, I'm gasping as the aftershocks of my orgasm tear through me. Without giving me a chance to recover, Kai lets go of my hair and helps me stand. He swivels the chair so it's facing Arthur and then sits down in it.

"Now my little slut, you're going to ride my cock. Face your husband. I want him to see your expression when I make you come again."

I obey immediately, facing away from Kai and sinking down on his cock slowly. His thick girth spreads me inch by delicious inch until he's fully inside me. Mmm, his cock feels so damn good. I've never been with anyone this big, and if I was selecting a guy to fuck based on his cock, Kai is a definite winner.

I raise my eyes to my husband and lock gazes with him. The look of raw need I see in his gaze shoots a bolt of desire through me, and I hook my legs around the outside of Kai's and start to rotate my hips slowly. I'm spread open to my husband's view, and I know he can see the base of Kai's cock before it disappears inside me. Kai's hand snakes around to play with my clit, and I moan loudly while holding on to the arms of the chair to give an experimental bounce on his cock.

Kai rubs my clit in just the right way to drive me crazy, and I speed up my bouncing and rocking as delight radiates from my pussy. I can feel my tits swaying with every movement, and I watch my husband as he enjoys the show. Arthur is rubbing harder against his pants, and I lick my lips, wishing he was inside my mouth right now while another guy was fucking me. My dirty thoughts push me closer to another orgasm, and my cries become needier and louder. I keep eye contact with Arthur, getting lost in the pleasure as I fuck myself on Kai's cock.

"Make him come inside you," Arthur groans out.

"Mmmm, yes," I whimper as I increase my pace.

Kai's fingers brush against my clit faster, and he plays with my nipple with his free hand. When he gives my nipple a sharp pinch, the pleasurable pain tips me over the edge. I cry out in ecstasy and clench around his cock as I'm wracked with rapture so intense stars sparkle along the edges of my vision.

Kai moves both his hands to my waist and holds onto me, forcing me up and down on his length. I'm chanting, "Oh god, oh god, oh god," from the intense joy as I rock faster and harder, trying to get Kai to come like my husband wants. I feel powerful with both men finding pleasure in what I'm doing, even if only one cock is inside me. This is fabulous.

"Ohhhh, god!" I cry out as I'm pushed into a sudden and unexpected orgasm. My legs shake and my eyes roll to the back of my head as Kai groans and explodes inside me. I can feel the warmth filling me, and knowing I'm taking a load of cum that isn't my husband's makes me feel so damn naughty.

I keep rocking on him until I can tell he's unloaded everything, and I slow the movements of my hips. He runs his hands up to cup both my breasts, his thumbs flicking lightly across my sensitive nipples. My breasts feel heavy and full, and I enjoy the moment of softness as I come down from my high.

Assuming we're done, I unhook my legs from him and make a movement to get up. Kai interrupts me.

"Get on your knees slut, it's time to clean up your mess."

Oooh, yes, please. I clamber off his lap, sinking to my knees between his legs. His cock is half hard and coated in our combined wetness. I run my tongue up his length, and he sucks in his breath. I dart my eyes up to his and then lean in to gently kiss the tip. He lets out an audible moan and runs his fingers along the sides of my head, tightening his grip slightly.

I continue cleaning off his cock. The salty tang of our mixed juices is pleasant, and I savor the way it mixes with his earthy aroma. Once he's clean, I turn my attention to his balls, lapping them while he groans in delight. I wish I could see Arthur, but I know he's watching, and I can feel my pussy tingling in excitement again.

The longer I work on Kai's cock and balls, the harder he gets. Mmm, maybe he'll fuck me again. To help make that happen, I take as much of his length in my mouth as I can. He's way too big to fit it all in, but I swirl my tongue along the underside of him and suck for all I'm worth.

He hisses and uses my hair to pull me off of him, groaning, "Such a good fucktoy. Your husband is a lucky man."

I blush at his words, oddly pleased. Arthur is lucky, and yet so am I. Not many husbands would be willing to let their wife play with another guy without feeling incredibly jealous.

Kai cups my chin and brushes his thumb across my lower lip and forces my mouth open. When he pushes his thumb into my mouth, I suck on it. There's something mesmerizing about being on my knees like this, and the world gets fuzzy around the edges again the longer I suck on his thumb.

When Kai speaks again, it takes me a moment to realize he's talking to my husband. "Have you changed your mind and want to do more than watch?"

Ohhhh. Desire courses through me, and I wonder if Arthur wants that. I don't even care if Kai fucks me again, I just want to give as much pleasure to my husband as I'm getting.

Arthur's voice sounds distant, but he seems hesitant. "I don't know..."

"All you have to do is ask," Kai chuckles.

My pulse speeds up, and I desperately want Arthur to say yes.

Arthur clears his throat. "Juliet, do you want that?"

Kai pulls his thumb out of my mouth so I can answer, and I rock back to rest on my heels. I have to look over my shoulder to see Arthur. The light from a torch next to him illuminates his expression. His eyes are dark and intent as he stares at me, and I can see he wants someone to give him permission to let go and take what is being offered.

My voice is throaty as I give him permission to explore. "Babe, I'm so fucking hot right now I need you. Whatever you want. I'm yours."

The tension breaks with my words when Arthur groans, "Then, yes."

When I look back at Kai, his eyes are sparkling and I can tell he's happy with the new development as he speaks. "So man, do you want her pussy or her mouth?"

"Pussy. I want to feel how much you stretched her."

A zing of pleasure ripples through me. Hearing that Arthur wants to fuck me after taking Kai's massive cock is so damn sexy.

Kai grins down at me. "Her pussy it is then. I'll take that beautiful mouth. She needs to swallow my cum this time."

I feel a spike of excitement, and I'm almost drunk on lust as I gaze up at Kai. "Yes, please."

Kai stands up and helps me to my feet. He pulls me over to where my husband is on the lounger. As if Arthur understands what the plan is, he unzips his jeans and pulls out his cock. It's fully erect, and a bead of precum is glistening on the end.

Oh, fuck yeah, I need that in me. No one needs to tell me what to do. I climb on the lounger with my husband, straddling his hips and gazing down at his face as I sink onto his cock. I'm still wet and swollen from so many orgasms, and Arthur's cock feels amazing. He's not as big as Kai, but he's a perfect fit for me. I moan and grind against him as Kai stands next to me, gripping the base of his cock. I turn my head and open my mouth as wide as I can, letting Kai feed me his dick. He slides into my throat as far as he can go while I grind against my husband's cock. My vision swims as the pleasure explodes through me. My body is a live wire of arousal, and I can't control my moans as I go wild on my husband's cock and hum around Kai's shaft in delight.

Kai wastes no time fucking my throat, holding onto the sides of my head for leverage. The added intensity of him face fucking me is perfection as I slam down on Arthur's cock and whimper with joy. Having my husband's cock inside me while my throat is full of another man is the dream I never even knew I had. I could do this all night—hell, I could take on an entire lineup of surfers like this. I'm feeling like a sexual goddess with two holes stuffed.

As I chase my orgasm, Arthur grasps my hips, bucking underneath me and urging me on. He whispers, "Come for me, baby."

His words push me over the edge, and my eyes close as I whine around the mouthful of Kai's cock. Waves of pleasure cascade through me, and Kai's cock muffles my moan. I don't get time to come down from my high before I peak again.

I writhe and explode as I hear Kai talking. "God, your wife is such a beautiful slut. I could fuck her mouth all night long."

Arthur thrusts up into me harder, sending shockwaves of euphoria through me. His fingers grip my waist, pulling me down as he groans, "I know. Fuck, baby, you feel so good. Oh god, I'm going to come."

I try to beg him to fill me, but all it comes out as is a mumble as Kai's thrusts speed up. Arthur's cock pulses, and he hisses, "Fuck!" as his body quivers and I feel his orgasm tear through him. I plant myself on his cock and grind against him as he fills me up. I'm reveling in the sensation of another load of cum in my pussy when Kai groans and spurts of his hot cum hit the back of my throat.

The taste of his seed sends me into overload, and my body shudders and spasms from the waves of ecstasy washing over me again and again. I feel like a mindless pleasure doll as Kai pulls out of my mouth as he finishes. I'm trembling violently as the aftershocks die down and Arthur wraps his arms around me, pulling me against him.

I close my eyes and sink into him, letting myself float in pure euphoria. I'm not sure how long it is until I can think again, but Arthur is rubbing my back gently when I finally can. Kai's sitting on the other lounge chair, drinking water.

I have no energy, but Arthur reaches for my glass of water and holds it for me. "Take a drink, baby."

I do, and the cool liquid refreshes me a little.

"You were amazing." Arthur says when he sets the glass back on the side table, and I can hear the awe in his voice.

I lift my head to meet his gaze. "Thank you for this."

I kiss him softly on the lips and then nestle against him once more. I'm exhausted and satisfied, and I just want to cuddle with my husband. The guys talk quietly as I drift, and when Arthur finally stirs, Kai helps me stand up.

Both the guys help me get dressed again, and I giggle. "We never went for that swim."

Kai laughs. "No, I didn't want your husband to miss any of the action."

Oh damn, I didn't even think about how Arthur wouldn't have seen much if we were in the water. That tells me Kai really does have experience with husbands watching.

Once we're presentable, Kai walks us through his house. I pause at the door and take his hand. "Thank you for a wonderful time tonight."

Kai flashes a bright smile, kissing both my cheeks. "Thank you too. Glad I ran into you at the bar."

I smile back and reach for Arthur, taking his hand. Arthur thanks him for a good night, and once we say our goodbyes, Arthur and I make our way down the rocky stairs and out to the beach.

I'm tired so we walk slowly through the sand, but I've never felt more connected to my husband. I glance up at Arthur. "This was the best adventure."

His answering smile is glorious and he pauses and tugs me against him, kissing my temple. "It was. I loved seeing you enjoying yourself with him, and the ending..."

He trails off and I can tell he's feeling shy about what happened, so I voice what I think he's feeling. "It was incredible."

"It was," he murmurs, and I wrap my arms around him and hold him tightly, understanding that what we did means he trusts me entirely. After a long moment, he leads me down the beach. We don't say another word, but the connection between us is as strong as ever and I know this trip changed the course of our lives for the better.

CHAPTER 5

Once we get home from Bali and we're unpacked and settled in, I remember the blog post Ariel sent me. I pull it up on my phone and smile at the title and read the rest.

Hotwives Unleashed: A Glimpse into a Taboo World

If you want to know what's wrong with the world, you don't have to look any further than your neighbor. We're surrounded by horny slutwives who are taking a cock in every hole by men other than their husband.

That's right, you'd be amazed at how many people are trying out the hotwife lifestyle. When you walk down the street, it's hard to stop thinking about what every couple you pass is doing behind closed doors. What depraved, filthy things are going on practically in your own backyard?

That friend you meet up with monthly for lunch? I bet she's a hotwife. She probably spends every Friday night on her knees, worshiping the cock of her husband's best friend while her husband sits across the room, stroking and watching. I bet she's feeling like a complete slut as the guy's cum fills her mouth until it's dripping down her chin, knowing that she's going to take another load, and another, and another, until she's nothing but a hole full of cum.

So the next time you're at the mall, think of that. Think of all the filthy, depraved things that are going on that shouldn't be. And you'll start to realize why this hotwife craze is such a problem.

Oh my god. I giggle as I type a message to Ariel.

I'm back and I just read Debra's blog. We're getting together this weekend for lunch, no excuses. I have so much to tell you and that post really is fucking hilarious. She sounds thirsty.

Since it's a workday, I know Ariel won't respond anytime soon. I set down my phone and giggle again as I think back to the night with Kai. I guess I'm now one of those depraved, horny sluts.

It's fucking wonderful.

The End

August Hotwife

Hotwife of the Month Book 8

Lacey Cross

Chapter 1

I need to start dinner, but instead, I'm standing in front of the fridge, staring at the calendar on the kitchen wall. My eyes land on the circled dates that mark my ovulation window. Ugh. I sigh heavily, feeling the familiar emotional rollercoaster that comes with trying to conceive.

"Hey, Will?" I call out, my voice wavering slightly. The muffled sounds of his engineering documentary drift from the living room.

"Yeah, babe?" he responds, his attention still divided.

I bite my lip, steeling myself. "It's...it's that time again. Ovulation window's coming up."

The TV goes silent. I hear William's footsteps approaching. He pauses in the doorway, and his hazel eyes meet mine, a mix of determination and weariness behind his glasses. I can see the toll this journey has taken on him too, the self-doubt that's been gnawing at him since we found out the fertility issues stem from his side because of a sports injury when he was younger.

"Already?" he asks, running a hand through his hair. "I swear it feels like we just finished the last round."

I nod, my throat tight. "I know."

My mind drifts to the countless doctors' appointments, the endless cycles of hope and disappointment. I want so desperately to be a mother, to fill our home with laughter and the joy of a child. But with each passing month, that dream seems increasingly out of reach.

William crosses the kitchen in two strides and wraps me in his arms. I breathe in his familiar scent, feeling his heartbeat against my cheek. Despite his own struggles, he's always been my rock, my steady support.

"It's just going to take time, Ariel," he murmurs, his voice a soothing rumble in his chest.

I want to believe him. I want to share in his unwavering faith, his analytical ability to see this as a problem we can solve together. But my heart is heavy with uncertainty. I rest my head on his shoulder, letting his warmth envelop me. "I just wish it wasn't so...clinical. Like we're scheduling intimacy instead of just letting it happen naturally."

William pulls back slightly, his hands cupping my face. His thumbs brush away the tears that have started to form in the corners of my eyes. "I know, sweetheart. It's tough. But we're in this together. And who knows? Maybe this time will be different."

I manage a small smile, appreciating his optimism. "You're right. We just have to keep trying." I take a deep breath, composing myself. "So, what's next? More documentaries while we wait for the right moment?"

He chuckles, a sound that lightens the mood slightly. "Well, I think we need to do something fun. How about we go out for dinner tonight? A little date night to remind us that there's more to our life than just...this."

A genuine smile spreads across my face. "That sounds wonderful."

He leans in, pressing his forehead against mine. "Good. Just keep the faith, baby. It will happen."

William and I settle into our seats at our favorite Italian restaurant, and I'm instantly glad we came out for dinner tonight. We needed this.

As we share a bottle of wine, I can tell there's something on his mind. He's got that look, the one where his eyebrows knit together just a fraction, and he's silent for a beat too long while he swirls his wine thoughtfully.

"You know how all our friends seem to be...experimenting with their relationships lately?" he finally asks, his voice low as if he doesn't want the table next to us to overhear.

I give him a playful grin, curious about where this is going. "You mean James and Marilyn? With the whole hotwife thing?" I reference our friends who recently opened up their marriage. Now more of our social circle is trying it, like it's catching. I try not to think about it too much. The idea is very appealing, but we've got bigger things to think about, like baby-making.

William nods, his gaze fixed on the ruby liquid in his glass. "Yeah, well, the idea of watching you with someone is crazy hot." He risks a glance at me, as if he's gauging my reaction.

Um, what? His comment is so unexpected it makes my heart skip a beat. A warm flush spreads across my cheeks as I process his words. William has always been the more cautious one in our relationship, his steady nature a counterpoint to my adventurous spirit. To hear him suggest something so daring sends a thrill through me, igniting a spark of excitement I didn't know was there.

My imagination races at the idea, vivid scenarios flashing through my mind. I picture William watching me with desire as another man's hands explore my body. A delicious tension coils in my stomach. The possibilities unfold in my mind as a newfound energy courses through my veins.

Fuck, I shouldn't want this. I toy with my napkin, trying to ignore how my entire body is awakening with desires I never knew I had.

"So you're saying you're into this?" I try to keep my tone steady so he can't see how turned on I'm getting.

He sets his wineglass down. "I've been thinking about it. A lot. And I wonder if it's something you'd ever consider trying."

A flush creeps up my neck. Given our current situation with trying to get pregnant, it seems like the worst possible timing. But my body doesn't care as my panties grow wet and a longing pulls at me deep in my core.

"Maybe we could discuss this in a few years, once we're past all this," I suggest, gesturing vaguely at my phone displaying the fertility tracking app on the lock screen.

He grows quiet, his eyes searching mine. "What if this could be part of the family planning?"

My heart skips another beat. "What do you mean?"

"I've been doing some reading. There are couples who've struggled with infertility, just like us, and they've found...creative solutions. Like bringing in a third party to help conceive."

I blink, trying to process his words. "You mean like a sperm donor and a turkey baster?"

He gives me a little smile and shakes his head. "Not exactly. More like...a known donor who's also a participant. Someone we both trust."

I'm stunned into silence, my mind whirling with the implications. When I find my voice again, I ask, "And who would that be?"

William looks at me with an intensity I haven't seen in years. "Zandar."

"Zandar?" I repeat while I try to gather my thoughts. Zandar is his best friend since childhood, and has always been supportive of us. The idea of him in this context is unexpectedly arousing. I imagine him stepping into our lives in ways we've never considered, and my body buzzes with illicit pleasure.

I first have to ask..."But not with a turkey baster?"

"NOT with a turkey baster," William confirms. "He's always been attracted to you. If everyone is comfortable, he could solve our problem."

I contemplate the magnitude of what he's proposing. It's unconventional and so damn hot. My nipples harden as I imagine fucking Zandar. I've heard through the grapevine that he's dominant in the bedroom. What would that be like?

William studies me, his eyes sparkling in the dim lighting, and my love for him eclipses the desire to fuck Zandar. As much as my inner slut wants to dance around the room and immediately agree to this, I need to make something clear.

I reach across the table and take his hand. "Don't suggest this just because you believe I'm unhappy. Our life together means everything to me. We can consider adoption in a couple of years if things don't work out.

He laughs and squeezes my hand. "I know, but this could be fun and turn into a win/win situation. But we don't have to decide anything tonight."

Desire radiates through me at his words, and I know I don't need more time. "If Zandar is open to it," I say slowly, trying to not sound like I'm ready for a celebration party, "then I'm interested."

William's eyes darken with lust. "I'll talk to Zandar about it."

Holy fuck, this might actually happen? I guess only if Zandar wants to, but still. William and I stare at each other for a minute, and an overwhelming surge of lust makes me desperate for my husband's cock.

My panties grow wetter and my pulse races as I pick up my fork. "Eat faster. We need to get home."

William grins. "I couldn't agree more."

We both shovel our food down while he signals to the server that we need our check. The drive home is torturous, with his hand on my bare thigh under my dress, caressing soft circles. With how turned on I am, I might come as soon as he slides inside me. There's a visible bulge in his pants, so I know we're on the same wavelength.

We don't even make it inside the house. Once we park and get out, William shuts the outer garage door and stalks me around the front of the car. He presses me against the side and cages me with his arms.

His eyes are filled with a hunger I haven't seen in years, and his voice is rough with desire. "You have no idea what you do to me, do you?"

A shiver runs down my spine, and I arch into him, desperate for more contact. "Show me."

He doesn't hesitate as his lips crash against mine in a searing kiss. His tongue delves into my mouth with a ferocity that steals my breath. I moan into the kiss, my hands fisting in his hair, pulling him closer.

William squeezes my breasts through my dress, his thumbs brushing over my hardened nipples. I gasp at the sensation, my hips rolling against him instinctively. It's crazy that just the thought of fucking Zandar makes me this desperate, but I love it.

He breaks the kiss, trailing his lips down my neck, nipping and sucking at the sensitive skin. "I want you," he growls against my pulse point. "Right here, right now."

"Do it," I moan.

He reaches down, hiking up my skirt, his fingers brushing against my soaked panties. I whimper and my head falls back against the car as he strokes my pussy through the damp fabric.

"Fuck, you're so wet," he groans, pressing a finger against my clit. "So ready for me."

"Yes," I hiss, grinding against his hand. "I need you inside me."

William hooks his fingers in my panties, dragging them down to my knees. I barely have time to register the cool air against my heated skin before he's plunging two fingers into my dripping core.

"God," he pants, his breath hot against my ear. "You feel so fucking good."

I cry out, my hips jerking as he pumps his fingers in and out of my pussy, his thumb circling my clit. My inner walls clench around him, drawing him deeper.

"That's it, baby. Let go. I've got you."

My orgasm crashes over me like a tidal wave, my body shaking with the force of it. I cling to William, my nails digging into his shoulders as I ride out the intense pleasure.

My vision goes white as I sob, "Oh God, William!"

He holds me close as I come down from my high, his fingers prolonging the bliss as he strokes my sensitive flesh. When I finally catch my breath, his eyes shine with pride and satisfaction.

"You're so beautiful when you come," he whispers, brushing a strand of hair from my face. "I could watch you all day."

I laugh, giddy from the pleasure, and tease, "And I'd let you. Now what about you? I need to see you come."

William grins, stepping back and swiftly removing his shirt. Oh shit, we're not moving inside? He kicks off his shoes and lowers his pants, freeing his cock.

"Come here," I beckon, crooking my finger at him. "Get that inside me."

There's a predatory gleam in his eye. "Your wish is my command," he says, lifting one of my legs and sliding his cock inside me.

We both groan from the pleasure as he fills me, and I cling to his shoulders as he pummels me against the car. This is a side of him I've never seen before. It's wonderful.

He sets a relentless pace, each thrust sending waves of pleasure coursing through me. The garage fills with the sounds of our panting and the raw, primal noise of our bodies colliding. Thank god he closed the outer door because in this moment, I wouldn't care if the entire neighborhood watched us.

The idea of me being that much of a slut thrills me, and my voice is breathy and desperate. "Harder. Fuck me harder!"

He growls, a sound that sends shivers down my spine, and his hips move faster, his cock plunging deeper. I can feel every inch of him, every ridge and vein as he strokes my inner walls, driving me towards another climax.

"You're so tight, so hot," he grunts, his face pressed against my neck.

His words and obvious pleasure send me spiraling, and I cry out as another orgasm rips through me. My body clamps down on his cock, pulsing and convulsing around him. He rides me through it, his own breath coming in ragged gasps.

"I'm close," he pants, his voice strained. "I want you to come again, baby."

My body hums with pleasure as he reaches between us, his fingers finding my clit and rubbing it in tight circles. The sensation is almost too much, and my oversensitive body spasms with each touch. He keeps me pinned against the car, his cock still drilling into me, his fingers insistent.

His voice is hoarse with effort. "Come for me. One more time. Let me feel you come all over my cock."

The relentless pressure on my clit sends me over the edge again. I scream his name, my body convulsing as a third climax tears through me. He groans, his hips jerking as his cock spasms, his warm cum coating me, and I can tell it was a powerful orgasm by the way he keeps shivering.

When he stops thrusting into me, we stand there for a moment, our bodies still joined. My mind spins from the pleasure. Holy fuck, that was amazing. Slowly, he withdraws, his hands gentle as he helps me straighten my clothes.

I lean against the car, my legs shaky. "That was..." I start, but words fail me.

"Yeah, it was," he agrees, leaning in to give me a soft kiss.

Hand in hand, we make our way into the house, the weight of our earlier conversation temporarily lifted. Tonight was so unexpected and so needed. I feel more connected to William than I have in months.

As we get ready for bed, I make my way to the kitchen for a glass of water. The calendar on the wall catches my eye. The circled dates no longer fill me with dread. Instead, there's a spark of hope, a glimmer of excitement. Maybe this unconventional path will lead us to the family we've always dreamed of.

As I curl up against William in bed, he wraps his arm around me, and a sense of peace washes over me. Tomorrow, we'll talk to Zandar and take the next step on this wild, unexpected journey.

CHAPTER 2

The next day, I'm afraid that all I'll be able to think about is my husband's offer, but luckily, work distracts me. It's half days at the elementary school this week, and as soon as my class is finished, the floodgates in my mind open up. I spend a couple more hours at work grading some papers, but I keep wondering what Zandar's cock looks like. He's incredibly attractive, but I've never let myself go there before.

The moment I walk in my front door, I kick off my shoes and curl up on the couch with my phone. I need a second opinion about whether this plan is crazy. It's time to call Sara.

Sara is one of my closest friends, and she knows all about this hotwife craze that is sweeping through our friends group. When she answers, I dive right in. "Hey, I need to run something past you. It's kind of a big deal."

There's a brief pause before Sara responds, her voice filled with concern. "Oh? What's up?"

I take a deep breath, trying to gather my thoughts. "So, William and I have been talking...we're considering something unconventional to help with our fertility struggles."

"Hmm, what do you mean, like a turkey baster? That's not that uncommon, you know. Fertility treatment is expensive."

I snort. Is that the first thing we all think of? "No, no, not a turkey baster...." I'm really not sure how to word what I want to say. Why didn't I plan my thoughts before calling her? After some hesitation, the words tumble out. "Okay, don't judge, but...we're going to ask my husband's friend to help us out."

There's a moment of silence before Sara responds, her voice calm and thoughtful. "But not with a turkey baster?"

Oh jeez. I giggle. "More of an organic insertion."

"Wow." She sounds surprised but also intrigued. "That's quite a step. How do you feel about it?"

I run my fingers through my hair. "Honestly? It's so far out of my comfort zone, but there's something about it that's thrilling."

Sara hums thoughtfully. "Well, it's not the craziest thing I've heard lately. You know how our friends keep saying being a hotwife has revitalized their marriage, and you have a double need."

"I know," I admit, twirling a strand of hair around my finger.

Sara's voice turns wistful. "I could never be a hotwife. I'm too self-conscious. But I really hope you have a wonderful time and get pregnant. I'll be cheering you on!"

Sara's lack of self-confidence has always surprised me, given that she's thin, blonde, and a knockout. But I've known her long enough to know it's not an act.

"Aw, Sara," I say, feeling a rush of affection for her. "I'm going to be hella self-conscious, too. The guys better be ready for one nervous first-time hotwife. Besides, this isn't really about being a hotwife; it's about having a baby."

Sara giggles and then squeals, "Ooooh, that reminds me. Check Debra's blog later. You'll love the latest post."

"I will," I laugh. Debra is another wife in our circle of friends, but she's been acting holier than thou and starting an anonymous blog about the dangers of the hotwife trend.

Just talking to Sara has eased my concerns. She obviously doesn't think me fucking someone else to get pregnant is a big deal.

"Now, promise me you'll keep me updated on how this all plays out," she says warmly.

"I will. I'll fill you in on all the details. Well, maybe not *all*."

Sara chuckles. "I'll be here for you, no matter what. Good luck."

As we hang up, I take a deep breath. Talking to Sara has helped me sort through my feelings. Now, all that's left is to find out if Zandar wants to fuck me. William better talk to him today. It's almost go-time, and I need a pussy full of cum asap. The thought sends a thrill through me. Oh god, I really hope this isn't a stupid plan.

I'm at the counter, chopping veggies for dinner, when William walks in, a massive grin on his face. He sweeps me into his arms, dips me like we're dancing, and kisses me so thoroughly that pleasure ripples through every nerve in my body. As we straighten up, he pulls me close, his voice a low rumble. "I talked to Zandar today."

"Oh, yeah?" I ask, heart pounding with excitement. "And? What did he say?"

William's grin widens, and he tightens his hold on me. "He's in. Said he's honored we trust him with this and promises to take good care of you."

A wave of relief rushes through me. "Wow, that's...big, isn't it?"

He chuckles. "Yeah, it is. He'll come over tomorrow. We'll have dinner, and then...we'll see where the night takes us."

I nod, biting my lip. "Okay, sounds good. As good as it can be, considering how crazy this is."

His expression softens, and he cups my cheek. "Hey, we don't have to do this if you're not comfortable."

I lean into his touch, feeling a surge of love for this man who's willing to go down this path with me. "I know, but I want to try."

He kisses my forehead. "Good, because I told him to call you filthy names."

What's this? I tip my head up and catch his smug grin. "Oh my god, you did not!"

"Mmm hmm, I told him to call you a dirty little slut and tell you he's going to breed you."

Lust simmers in my gut, and I have a hard time responding. "You're terrible," I whisper, playfully swatting his chest, though the heat in my cheeks betrays my excitement. "But that's...really hot."

William laughs. "I thought you might like that. We need to make this as enjoyable for you as possible, right?" His hands slide down to my hips, pulling me closer. "Zandar is...quite enthusiastic."

I raise an eyebrow, feeling a flutter of anticipation. "Really?"

He hums in response. "Yep, and I think he's the perfect choice."

Oh god, tomorrow can't get here fast enough. I push out of his arms and turn back to the counter, chopping veggies with a renewed sense of purpose. The thought that I might become pregnant makes this plan even more erotic.

The rest of the evening passes in a blur of quiet anticipation. We eat dinner and watch a movie, but my mind is anywhere but the present. I keep imagining what it will be like to fuck someone other than William.

Later, as we lie in bed with William's arm draped protectively around me, I can't help but whisper into the darkness, "William?"

"Mm hmm?" he murmurs sleepily.

"I love you."

His voice is warm and reassuring. "I love you too. More than anything."

I snuggle in closer to him and try to get some sleep. Tomorrow is going to be a big day.

CHAPTER 3

My mind is a scattered mess as I try to work the next day. Thank god it's another half day at school. By the time I get home, all I can think about is fucking Zandar. I'm too worked up to do anything productive. As I change out of my work clothes and put on shorts and a t-shirt, I contemplate my afternoon. Hmm, maybe my husband needs a distraction at work. I plop down at the kitchen table and text him.

Ariel

> I can't stop daydreaming about tonight.

He replies immediately.

William

> Me either.

Butterflies swirl in my stomach. What would he say if I told him I've been imagining fucking Zandar all day? Let's find out!

Ariel

> I have a confession...

William

> Yes?

I bite my lip, nervous about what his reaction will be.

Is it bad that I'm getting worked up by the thought of fucking Zandar beyond just making a baby?

He doesn't answer for a full minute, and my anxiety skyrockets. When his text comes through, there's a picture attached. It's of him sitting in our car in the parking lot of his work, but the camera is angled down towards his crotch, showing a very visible bulge in his pants.

Babe, this isn't because I've been thinking about you getting pregnant.

A wave of heat crashes over me as a sudden surge of arousal makes me squirm in my seat. Holy fuck, he really *does* want to share me. My heart hammers as I type.

Oh my god, how are you working today?

It's hard...

Ha ha, I married a funny guy.

I'm so wet right now. If you're going to change your mind, do it now before I get even more worked up.

While I wait for his reply, I can't resist the urge to touch myself, slipping a hand down the front of my shorts. My fingers brush against my already soaked panties as my clit throbs. I feel like such a slut for telling him how wet I am for his friend, but it's also freeing. Is this what our friends mean when they say being a hotwife is revitalizing their marriage? I definitely feel naughtier, and want to tell William all my dirty fantasies.

I'm not changing my mind. I've been thinking about

Fuck, that's hot. I moan as I press down and rub my pussy harder through the fabric of my panties, trying to get the friction where I need it most.

He sends me another message while I'm distracted.

William

I picture Zandar, his dark skin glistening with sweat as he drills into me. God, I hope tonight goes well. But beyond that, I'm enjoying this new-found dirty side of my husband. My hand is busy, so I use speech-to-chat for my next message.

Ariel

William

The mental image is so vivid that it short circuits my brain. I don't even realize what I'm doing when I push my panties aside. I'm lost in the fantasy as I rub tight circles over my clit. My orgasm builds in record time...until the ding of another text message brings me back to focus.

William

Ugh, he knows me too well. I pull my hands out from between my legs and wipe my fingers on my tank top.

Now would I do that?

I give him an emoji of a face with a halo.

Don't make me call it off with Zandar tonight.

As if. I giggle as I type back.

I'm being good. I just need it to be after dinner already.

I sigh at William's next text.

Soon, baby. Soon.

Yeah, not goddamn soon enough. We text back and forth for the next couple of hours until I tell him I'm going to take a long shower and I promise to be good. Maybe tonight I'll get an amazing orgasm and become pregnant. That would be a total win.

When William comes home and walks into the bedroom, the look in his eyes tells me he's ready to ravish me. I'm pulling on my favorite hot pink dress, though I'm not really sure why I'm dressing up since it's just coming off again soon. But a big part of me wants to look sexy tonight. William stalks towards me, and I put my hand out to stop him, pressing on his chest so he can't get too close.

"Hey, now," I purr at him. "You can kiss me, but that's all. Promise?"

He and I both know he could have me bent over the bed, my dress at my waist, and him balls deep in me in one minute flat if he really wanted.

He groans, "Such a little tease."

I relent and move into his arms, brushing my lips against his. When he tries to deepen the kiss, I push him back with a laugh. "Hey now, behave."

Putting distance between us, I move over to the mirror to adjust my dress. The way the fabric clings to my curves makes it clear I'm not wearing a bra, and the hem is short enough that the lacy edge of my thigh-high stockings peeks out.

While William changes out of his work clothes, I watch him in the mirror. The bulge in his pants is unmistakable. Knowing William is turned on, along with me being in my fertile window, makes tonight way more erotic than I expected.

I'm about ready to flirt with him some more to torture us both when the doorbell rings. A zing of pleasure ripples through me. It's time!

CHAPTER 4

Zandar brought Thai food with him, but all I can do is sit there and pick at it. The aroma of spices and coconut milk normally would tempt me, but I'm too excited. Across from me, Zandar's vivid green eyes lock onto mine, and heat rises in my cheeks. His gaze is intense, searching, and I find myself unable to look away. I've never paid much attention to my attraction to other people before. Sure, I always thought Zandar was sexy, with his chiseled jawline and broad shoulders, but I'm not going to drool over my husband's friends. At least, I never used to.

Now everything is different, and the air between us is charged. Whenever he looks at me, I get a rush of desire, and my skin tingles with awareness. I shift in my seat, trying to find a comfortable position that doesn't betray my growing arousal.

Zandar takes a bite of his food, and I watch as his lips close around the fork. I swallow hard, my mouth suddenly dry. The simple act of him eating shouldn't affect me this way, but it does. I force myself to look down at my plate, my fingers fidgeting with my fork.

William sits to my right, his hand resting casually on my thigh, his fingers tracing slow, deliberate patterns that send tingles up my spine. His hand is warm, and it's like he's leaving trails of fire on my skin. How can such a simple touch be so distracting? I'm sure he knows exactly what he's doing, and he's just trying to keep me needy.

The conversation flows easily while we eat, but there's an undercurrent, a tension that has my body thrumming with anticipation.

"So, Ariel," Zandar says, his voice a deep, velvet purr that seems to wrap around me. "I've heard you have quite the appetite tonight."

His eyes hold mine, the implication in his words hanging thick in the air. The corner of his mouth quirks up in a small smile, and the flutter in my stomach has nothing to do with hunger. My mind is racing with responses. Three sexual innuendos fly through my brain, each more daring than the last. Why is it so hard to flirt with Zandar? I've never been this uncertain around him before. William gives my thigh a gentle, reassuring squeeze, and his support helps me loosen up a little.

I give Zandar a playful smile. "Well, you know me, always ready for a feast. And I have a feeling you're serving up something...delectable."

Oh god, that sounded dumb. Didn't it? This is what happens when it's been years since you've flirted with anyone but your husband.

Zandar's eyes darken. "Is that right? You have an appetite that needs satisfying?" His voice is a low growl, filled with a promise that sets my heart racing.

Hey now, I guess he appreciates my awkward flirting. I swear, if he keeps looking at me like that, I'm going to melt right here. I try to keep my composure as I whisper, "Yes."

"And what exactly are you hungry for? Tell me. Let me hear you say it."

His eyes never leave mine, the intensity of his gaze making it difficult to think clearly. He's enjoying my reaction to him, isn't he?

I glance at William, who nods encouragingly, his hand inching closer and closer to my pussy. Yeah, he's trying to drive me crazy as well.

My voice is steadier than I expect. "I'm hungry for you to fill me up."

He hums contentedly. "That's what I like to hear. Now eat up. You need your strength."

Like I'm going to be able to eat after that? I give it my best effort, and the guys chat and joke around about their college days while I manage a few more bites. By the time we're finished, I'm practically aching with need. I can't believe what we're all about to do, but god, I want this.

Zandar stands, extending his hand. I take it, and a jolt of electricity passes between us as he helps me to my feet. "Let's go fill that pussy full of cum and make a baby."

I laugh at how direct he's being, and William grabs a chair from the table and follows us to the bedroom. I didn't consider where William was going to sit while he watched, and him bringing his own chair is filthy in such a good way.

In the bedroom, Zandar turns to me. "Are you ready to be a good little slut tonight?" he asks, his voice a deep rumble that sends shivers down my spine.

Oh god, if he keeps talking dirty, he's going to melt my brain. "I'm ready. I'm so ready."

He smiles and cups my chin, his thumb brushing over my lower lip. "Good. Because I'm going to make you beg for my cum."

My brain blips out and my cheeks flush at his words. I can't look away from him. His gaze holds me captive, and honestly, I don't want to escape.

William places the chair in the corner of the room, his presence a silent support, a reminder that he's there, watching, approving. I never imagined I'd be this turned on by fucking someone while William watched, but suddenly I understand why all my friends are becoming hotwives. When your husband is into it, it's fucking amazing.

Zandar's hand slides down, tracing the curve of my neck, the line of my shoulders. His touch is feather light and makes me shiver. He might treat me gently, but I can tell he's fully in control and he could turn demanding at any moment.

He leans in, his lips brushing against my ear, his voice a husky whisper. "First, I want you to show me what you've got. Strip for us. Slowly."

Strip? Right. I can do that. My hands tremble slightly as I reach for the hem of my dress, my fingers toying with the fabric. I want to tease them and drive them crazy, just like they were doing to me through dinner.

I pull the dress up slowly, inch by inch, revealing more skin. I'm breathless and my nipples harden as Zandar's eyes follow every movement, his gaze a tangible caress. William shifts in his chair and hums in approval. I never knew stripping in front of two men would be this erotic, but just knowing I have their full attention is powerful.

When the dress is finally over my head, I drop it to the floor, and I stand there in my bra, panties, garter belt and stockings. I'm feeling an odd mix of vulnerable yet also like a sexual goddess. I've never felt so desired, so wanted.

Zandar takes a step back, his eyes roaming over my body. "Beautiful," he murmurs, almost to himself. "Now, spin. Let me see all of you."

I obey, turning slowly and blowing a kiss at William as I circle past him. I just want Zandar to fuck me, so him toying with me and making me do his bidding is torture. Sweet, delicious torture.

When I face Zandar again, his eyes are dark with desire. He wants me. Knowing that I'm affecting him is intoxicating.

"Now, let's see if you taste as delicious as you look," he growls as he pushes me back onto the bed. He unhooks the garters and slowly rolls my stockings down each leg, his fingers trailing along my skin, leaving goosebumps in their wake. I prop myself up on my elbows, watching him as he tosses the stockings aside and kisses his way up my leg. His stubble scratches lightly against my skin, adding a delicious friction that makes me shiver.

I glance over at William, who is seated comfortably in the chair, his eyes locked on us. He smiles at me, a slow, encouraging smile that tells me he's loving the show and sends a wave of heat through me.

Zandar's mouth reaches the apex of my thighs, his breath hot against my pussy, still covered by my panties. He looks up at me, a wicked gleam in his eyes. "You're already so wet. I can smell your arousal."

He hooks his fingers into the waistband of my panties and peels them down, inch by agonizing inch. I raise my knees to make it easier for him to remove them, and when he tosses them aside, I'm completely exposed to him. Everything we're doing is so fucking naughty–in such a good way.

Zandar pushes my legs further apart and leans in, his tongue flicking out to taste me. I gasp, my hips jerking involuntarily. Ooooh god, I really didn't expect him to go down on me. I guess he's not going to fuck me quickly and unload his seed.

His voice vibrates against my sensitive flesh as he dives in, murmuring, "Mmm, you taste incredible." He explores every fold, every crease, until he finds my clit and circles it slowly.

I writhe under his talented tongue as the pressure builds like a coil tightening in my belly. Zandar slides a finger inside me, then another, pumping slowly in time with the movements of his tongue. I moan, my eyes fluttering closed, the sensation overwhelming as I rush towards my orgasm.

I hear William's sharp intake of breath from the corner, and it reminds me he's there, watching me come undone. I moan in pleasure from Zandar's tongue and the knowledge that William is enjoying this—that he wants this for me. For us.

Zandar's fingers curl inside me, hitting that perfect spot, and the delight is too much. I cry out, my orgasm crashing over me like a wave. My body convulses, my hips bucking against his mouth, but he doesn't stop. He rides out the storm, his tongue and fingers working in tandem, wringing every last drop of pleasure from me.

As I come down from the high, Zandar sits up, his lips glistening with my juices. He grins, a satisfied, predatory smile. "Ready for more, slut?"

I nod, breathless, my body already aching. William is leaning forward in his chair, rapt. He nods his silent approval for us to continue.

Zandar stands as he yanks off his shirt, revealing his muscular, well-defined chest, dusted with a light sprinkling of dark brown hair. His dark skin seems to glow in the soft light, highlighting his features. He takes his time, his movements deliberate and confident, allowing me to appreciate his chiseled physique.

He undoes his belt next, the leather sliding through the loops of his jeans with a subtle hiss. He pops the button, the zipper following with a tantalizing hum. His dark jeans slide down his lean, muscular legs, leaving him in nothing but a pair of form-fitting boxer briefs that cling to his powerful thighs. Fuck, he's driving me insane.

His boxers are the last thing he's wearing, and when he removes them, I have to fight the urge to lick my lips. Mmmm, yummy. His cock is thick and long, the head smooth and slightly larger than the shaft. His balls are equally impressive, hanging low and full. I know that bigger balls don't mean better fertility, but I still get a zing of pleasure at the thought of him unloading inside me.

"On your hands and knees, slut," Zandar commands, his voice thick with need. "I'm going to fuck you from behind and fill that pussy full of cum."

Mmm, about damn time. I quickly get on all fours and wiggle my ass at the guys while looking over my shoulder at William. His eyes are hooded and his hand is stroking his cock through his jeans. I can see the lust in his eyes, the desire. The love.

Zandar positions himself behind me, his hands grasping my hips. He rubs the head of his cock against my entrance, teasing me, making me whimper with need. I try to push back against him, but he pulls back, denying me the satisfaction I crave.

"Please," I beg and rock my hips, wishing he'd slip his cock inside me. "Please fuck me."

He chuckles, a low, throaty sound that sends shivers down my spine. "Oh, you want this cock?" he asks, rubbing the tip against my clit, making me gasp. "Does the slut want me to fill her up?"

Fuck, him talking to me this way is making me even more desperate.

"Yes," I moan, "Please, I need it. I need you."

He leans down, his body covering mine, his lips brushing against my ear. "You need me to breed you?" he growls. "You want me to fill this tight little pussy with my cum?"

His words send a surge of desire coursing through me as the ache in my core grows more insistent. "Yes," I whimper. "Breed me. Fill me with your cum."

He groans, his grasp on my hips tightening. "Such a good girl," he praises, his voice thick with lust. My mind blanks at being called a good girl, and I barely have time to process it before he slams into me, balls deep.

I cry out, my back arching as he immediately begins to thrust vigorously, his hips slapping against my ass. His cock is hitting all the right spots, and another orgasm builds quickly. He's not being gentle, and I glory in the roughness as he quickens his pace.

"You feel so fucking good," he groans. "I can't wait to fill this pussy full of cum...breed you...make you pregnant."

Oh god, that's hot. His words send me spiraling, and I explode, my body convulsing around his cock. As I shudder from my orgasm, he pulls out and flips me onto my back. Within seconds, he's driving into me again.

"I want to see you," he grunts, his hips moving like pistons. "I want to watch you take every last drop of me."

I'm desperate now, my nails clawing at his back, my feet digging into the mattress as I meet his thrusts, urging him deeper. "Please, Zandar," I beg, my voice ragged. "Oh god, please. Fill me. Breed me. I need it."

He groans as he jackhammers into me erratically, his body tensing. But instead of letting go, he slows down, pulling out of me and rolling me onto my side. He lifts my leg, opening me up to him, and slides back in, his cock hitting new spots inside of me.

"Fuck," I gasp, my body shuddering with pleasure.

"You like that, don't you?" he growls, his hand gripping my thigh, holding me in place. "You like it when I fill you up, when I fuck you deep?"

"Yes," I moan, my body trembling with every thrust. "God, yes."

He moves his hand to my clit, rubbing it in time with his thrusts, driving me wild. Pleasure builds in layers as I spiral towards another orgasm.

"Come for me," he commands. "Come all over my cock. Milk me."

His words push me over the edge, and I come hard, my body convulsing around him, my screams filling the room. But he doesn't stop, doesn't slow.

"Fuck, you're so tight," he groans, his hands digging into my hips.

His cock swells inside of me and his body tenses as he gets closer to his own release. But he's not ready to let go yet, not until he's wrung every ounce of pleasure from me.

He withdraws again, flipping me onto my back and spreading my legs wide. He slides back in, his eyes locked onto mine, his body trembling with the effort to hold back.

I'm crazed from the pleasure, and I babble. "Breed me, oh god, please, breed me. Need your cum. Please!"

Right before he comes, he pulls out. Holy hell? How can he deny himself like this? His body shudders from how close to coming he is, and his cock glistens with our combined juices. Wetness leaks out of me, and I know I look well fucked.

"God," he murmurs, his voice still thick with desire. "You're so fucking beautiful when you come."

He leans down and kisses me, his tongue exploring my mouth, tasting me. His cock surges against my thigh, as if protesting that he hasn't come yet.

"I want more," he growls. "I want to fuck you in every position, in every way. I want to fill you with my cum until you're overflowing with it."

Pleasure swirls in my core, and I moan, "Yesss."

He gives me a wicked smile. "Good, because I'm not done with you yet."

He stands up, his cock hard and ready, and I can't help but stare at it. My mouth waters with desire as he reaches down, grabbing my ankles, and pulls me to the edge of the bed. He spreads my legs wide, exposing my pussy.

"You're so wet," he groans, his fingers tracing the edges of my pussy lips. "So ready for me."

My mind is totally fucked and I'm unable to do anything but whimper as he positions himself at the entrance of my eager pussy. With a slow, deliberate thrust, he enters me, his cock filling me up, stretching me to the limit. I gasp, my eyes rolling back in my head as he bottoms out.

Zandar sets a quick pace, his hips driving into mine with a rhythm that sends waves of pleasure crashing over me. I'm lost in the sensation, my body responding instinctively to his touch. Each thrust pushes me closer to the edge, my orgasm building inside me like a storm.

William moves in closer, reaching for my breast and teasing my nipple. The sensation sends shockwaves through my body, and I moan more loudly, my pussy clenching around Zandar's cock.

"Fuck," Zandar grunts. "So good."

I'm beyond caring about anything but getting his cum, and I whimper, "I want you to breed me, put a baby in me."

His eyes darken with desire, and he picks up the pace, his cock pounding into me with a ferocity that borders on primal. I can feel him getting closer, his body tensing as he approaches his own release.

"Oh, yeah?" he grunts. "Think of how full your belly is going to be when I'm done with you."

Oooh, god. I imagine finally being pregnant and my stomach swelling. I want it so badly.

He continues the dirty talk as he fucks me. "You're so desperate for this, aren't you?"

I writhe under him, mewling out, "Yes!"

"I'm going to fill you up. You're going to be such a pretty mess when I'm done with you. His voice is strained with lust. "Here it comes."

With a final, powerful thrust, he groans as thick spurts of cum coat my inner walls. I can imagine all his little swimmers rushing to their destination, and my head spins as his cock pulses, unloading every last drop. The sense of fullness is overwhelming, and I swear his cum is flooding my womb.

He gives one final whack against my pussy and then collapses on the bed next to me, spent. A zing of pleasure ripples down my spine as his cum leaks out of me. God, this is naughty.

When William moves his hand to my stomach, I realize he's still with us by the bed. His palm is warm as he rubs circles on my belly and leans down to kiss me.

"That was fucking hot," he whispers against my lips. "I love you."

"I love you too." I smile, my body humming with pleasure, my heart full.

I'm not sure the last time I was so thoroughly fucked, and I mentally drift as Zandar stirs. He sits up, the muscles in his back rippling as he runs a hand through his tousled hair. He smiles at me before he stands up and gathers his clothes from the floor. I admire his body as he dresses. It's so damn dirty to know I was just fucking him.

When Zandar is dressed, the men help me to the center of the bed and William says, "I'll be right back, babe."

Zandar turns to me and says, "Thank you for everything. Tonight was wonderful."

"It was. Thank you too," I murmur, and he waves goodbye and follows William out of the room.

I'm left alone in the room, the scent of sex and sweat still lingering in the air. I stretch out on the bed, my body humming with satisfaction as their footsteps recede down the hallway. I hear the faint murmur of their voices, and then the soft click of the front door closing.

When William gets back to the room, there's a hunger in his gaze, a possessiveness that makes my heart race. He quickly removes his clothes and climbs onto the bed, his hands reaching for me, his touch gentle yet firm.

He rolls me onto my stomach, his hands tracing the curve of my spine, sending shivers of anticipation down my body. He knows I love this position, and it's just like him to be thinking of me when it's his turn for pleasure.

His cock presses against my ass, hard and insistent. I push back against him, eager for more, my body already coming alive again. He leans down, his lips blazing a trail of kisses along my shoulder and the nape of my neck, his breath hot and ragged.

He enters my pussy, slowly at first, teasingly, before withdrawing slightly, making me gasp with desire. Then he plows into me, fierce and deep, filling me completely. I cry out, my fingers clutching at the sheets, my body already so close to the edge again.

His body covers mine, his weight pressing me into the mattress. His lips brush against my ear, his breath coming in hot gasps. "You're mine," he growls, his voice thick with lust. "All mine."

"Yours," I whimper as he moves, each thrust deliberate and powerful, claiming me. I match his rhythm, pushing back against him.

He continues to kiss my neck, my shoulders, his teeth grazing my skin, each touch sending waves of pleasure coursing through me. Each thrust feels like a declaration of love as the pleasure builds.

"Oh, god, I love you," I moan, my body trembling as I climb higher and higher.

His movements become more urgent at my words, his body driving into mine with an uncontrollable need. Finally, with a cry that echoes through the room, I reach the peak, my body convulsing with ecstasy.

He follows soon after, his body stiffening, his hips pushing against mine one last time as he explodes, filling my pussy with the second load of cum for the night.

We collapse together, spent and sated. Yep, I just got fucked out of my mind. What a way to live.

Right before I fall asleep, he kisses my forehead, murmuring, "I love you so much."

I mumble, "I love you too," and then I'm out like a light.

CHAPTER 5

The next morning, my body aches in such a glorious way. Yeah, I need to take it easy today. When I wander into the kitchen, I pour myself a cup of coffee and sit at the table before pulling up Debra's latest blog post.

Hotwives Unleashed: A New Trend in Baby-Making?

Listen to what I've been hearing through the grapevine lately. It seems like there's a new trend among those desperate to conceive, and it's not just turkey basters and fertility clinics anymore. Oh no, dear readers, it's much more scandalous than that. Women are using the excuse of "needing to get pregnant" to dip their toes into the hotwife lifestyle. Can you even believe it?

I mean, let's consider this for a second. Imagine that sweet couple down the street, the ones who have been trying for a baby for what feels like forever. You might assume they're spending their nights poring over ovulation charts and temperature graphs, right? Wrong! They're inviting other men into their bedroom, all in the name of "fertility assistance." I bet she's spreading her legs wide, offering her ripe, eager pussy to her husband's best friend, begging him to fill her with his potent seed.

Picture this: She's on her hands and knees, her back arched, presenting herself like an animal in heat. Her husband is sitting in the corner, watching with rapt attention as his friend—let's call him Steve—positions himself behind her. Steve's hands grip her hips, his thick cock poised at her slick entrance. "You want this, don't you, slut?" he growls, his voice thick with lust. "You want me to breed you, to fill this tight little pussy with my cum?"

She moans, pushing back against him, desperate to get him inside her. "Yes, please. I need it. I need you to breed me," she begs, her voice ragged with desire. Her husband's eyes are hooded, his hand stroking his own cock as he watches his wife about to be claimed by another man.

Steve drills into her, his cock filling her completely. She cries out, her body trembling with pleasure. He begins to move, his hips slapping against her ass, his cock sliding in and out of her wet, eager pussy. "Fuck, you feel so good," he grunts, his fingers digging into her flesh. "I can't wait to fill you with my cum, to make you pregnant."

Her husband groans from the corner, his eyes never leaving the sight of his wife being fucked, being bred. He's enjoying this, getting off on the sheer depravity of it all.

But let's not kid ourselves, dear readers. This isn't just about making babies. This is about lust, plain and simple. These women aren't just trying to conceive—they're using any excuse to become hotwife sluts.

To use the act of conception as an excuse for such lewd behavior is truly depraved. I would never, ever, even think about wanting such filthy things. I'm just a concerned citizen, a moral observer, reporting on the scandalous trends sweeping through our neighborhoods. I'm just here to tell you, dear readers, that the hotwife lifestyle is alive and well, and it's hiding behind the most innocent of excuses.

So the next time you see that sweet couple down the street, the ones who have been trying for a baby, just remember: they might be indulging in their wildest fantasies, exploring their darkest desires, all in the name of "fertility assistance." And who knows? Maybe they're crossing lines that should never be crossed. Let us be grateful for our own moral fortitude. I, for one, will continue to buck this hotwife trend.

I nearly choke on my coffee, laughter bubbling up. Oh god, how did she hear the news so fast? William must have told one of his friends. I don't mind that he did, and the whole situation amuses me.

William walks in as I'm chuckling. "What's so funny?" he asks, pouring himself a cup.

"Just Debra being her usual self," I say and quickly text Sara that if I weren't already a hotwife, Debra would make me want to be one. I set my phone down, turning my attention to William.

He joins me at the table, and we sip our coffee in comfortable silence for a moment. Then, my expression turns serious. "Last night was incredible, but what if I don't get pregnant this time?"

William sets down his cup, reaches across the table, and takes my hand. His eyes are warm, filled with affection. "Then," he says, his voice low and teasing, "Zandar will just have to keep fucking a baby into you until you are."

My eyes widen, and I let out a laugh, as a blush creeps up my cheeks. "Is that a promise?" I ask, a playful note in my voice.

"It's more than a promise, Ariel. It's a guarantee."

A thrill runs through me at his words, and a warmth spreads through my body. Baby-making, it turns out, is sounding better and better.

The End

ABOUT LACEY CROSS

Lacey Cross is a wife-sharing erotica writer with over 100 short stories published since she started in 2021. Her stories emphasize the pleasure found from the wife living her best slut life and embracing the hotwife lifestyle. She explores themes of free use, submissive wives with dominant bulls, BDSM... and oh-so-many men.

Find her books, erotic shorts, and audiobooks on her website: https://lacey-cross.com/

If you like romantic BDSM erotica, check out her April Cross books at: https://april-cross.com/

www.ingramcontent.com/pod-product-compliance
Lightning Source LLC
Chambersburg PA
CBHW030005010826
48973CB00009B/2667